This Book Belongs To:

KEEP
MUSIC
REAL.

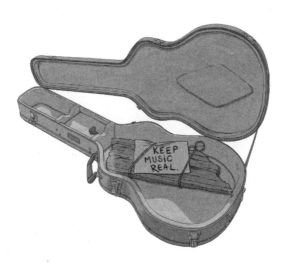

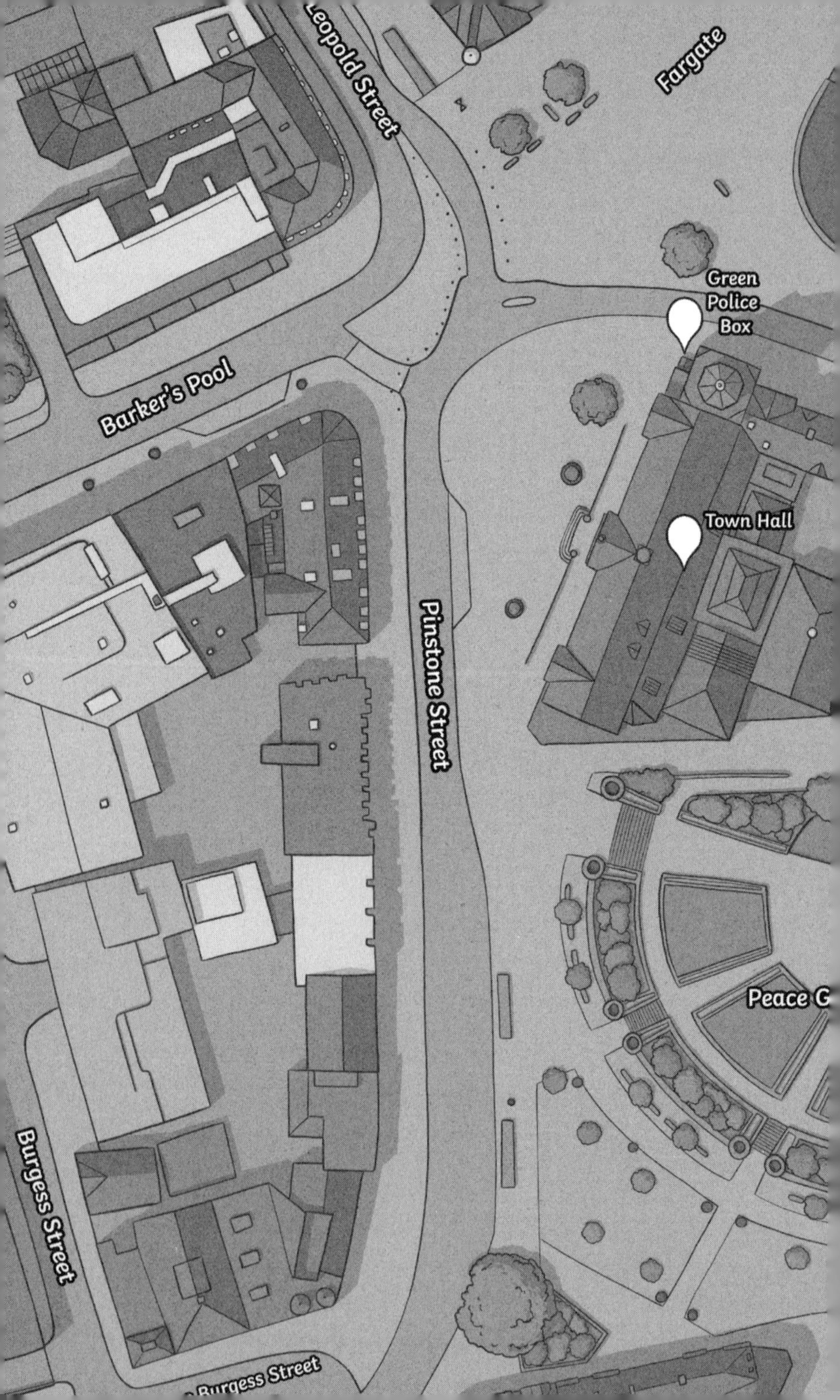
Leopold Street
Fargate
Green
Police
Box
Barker's Pool
Town Hall
Pinstone Street
Peace G
Burgess Street
Burgess Street

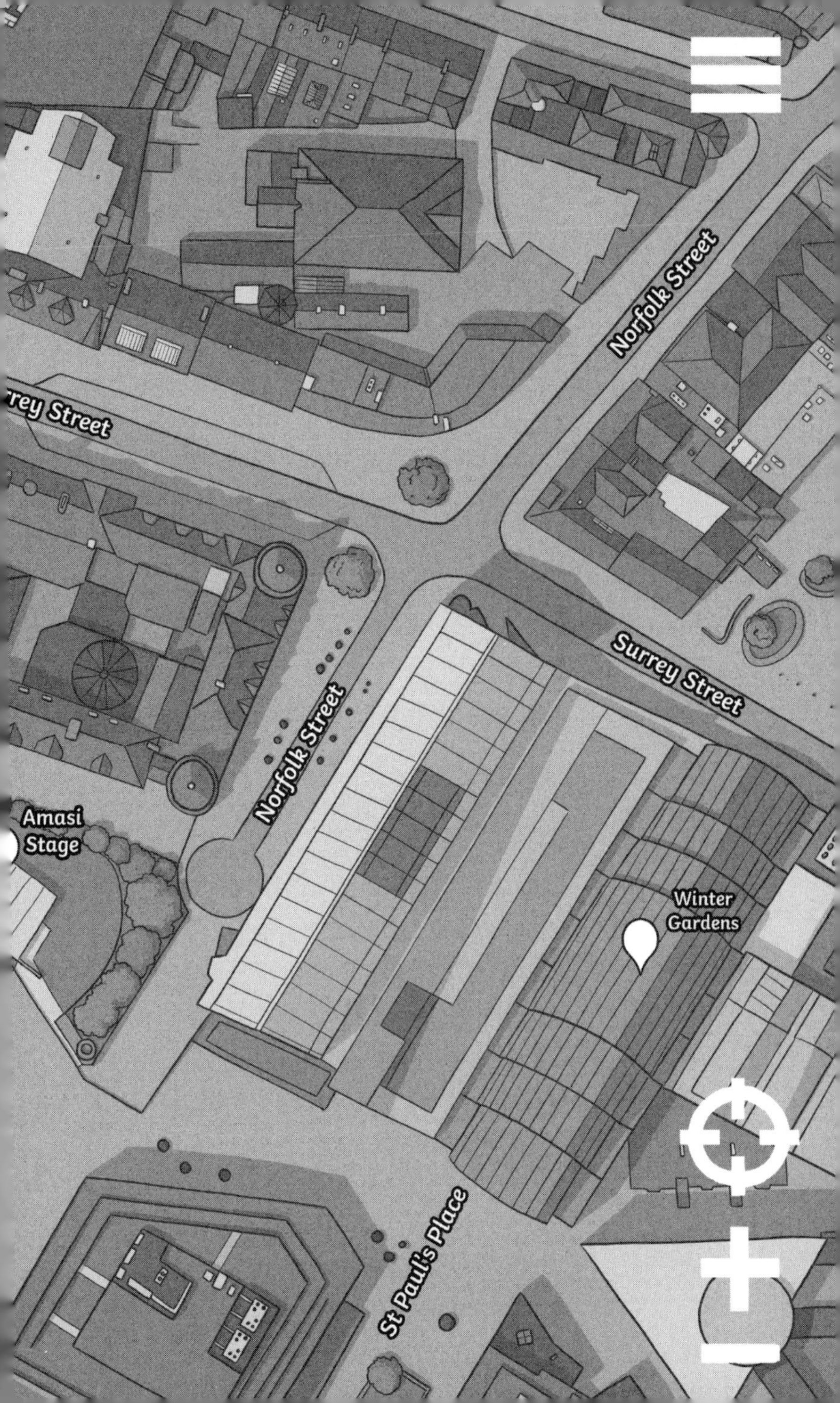

rrey Street
Norfolk Street
Surrey Street
Norfolk Street
Amasi Stage
Winter Gardens
St Paul's Place

First published 2022 © Twinkl Ltd of Wards Exchange,
197 Ecclesall Road, Sheffield S11 8HW

ISBN: 978-1-914331-44-2

MIX
Paper from
responsible sources
FSC® C022913

We're passionate about giving our children a sustainable future, which is why
this book is made from Forest Stewardship Council® certified paper.
Learn how our Twinkl Green policy gives the planet a helping hand at
www.twinkl.com/twinkl-green.

Printed in the United Kingdom.

10 9 8 7 6 5 4 3 2 1

A catalogue record for this book is available from the British Library.

Twinkl is a registered trademark of Twinkl Ltd.

A TWINKL ORIGINAL

THE CURIOUS CASE OF THE STOLEN SHOW

Twinkl Educational Publishing

Contents

Chapter One 1

Chapter Two 11

Chapter Three 19

Chapter Four 30

Chapter Five 37

Chapter Six 44

Chapter Seven 51

Chapter Eight 58

Chapter Nine 65

Chapter Ten 71

Chapter Eleven 79

Chapter Twelve 88

Chapter Thirteen 97

Chapter Fourteen 104

Chapter Fifteen 109

Chapter Sixteen 117

Chapter Seventeen 122

Chapter Eighteen 131

Chapter Nineteen 141

Chapter One

As far as Saturdays tend to go, this is going to be one of the most exciting ever!

I've worked out that I've been alive for five hundred and ninety-eight Saturdays so far. How cool is that? I'm officially coming up to my six hundredth Saturday. I don't think any of them have been as awesome as this one is going to be, though. I'm going to see my favourite singer performing, for real, in the flesh, in a massive concert. Not just that but we're going to a tour launch event first. You see, the concert is the opening of Amasi's new world tour, right back here in our home city. She's from Sheffield, too, just like me. That's just one of a hundred reasons why I love her.

"Demi! Are you ready?"

That'll be one of my dads shouting upstairs. I don't know why he thinks he needs to shout – it's not like we live in a big house. You can hear every floorboard creak from every other room, no matter where you are, and I think the walls must be made out of cardboard. I don't know why he's asking if I'm ready, either. It's quarter past eight and, obviously, I've been up and ready for about two and a half hours. I was way too excited to sleep. All of my clothes were laid out last night. I know I didn't need to be up so early but I've literally been bouncing around ever since. I can feel my breakfast cereal swishing about in my tummy.

I know I said 'one of my dads' just then. I've got two dads but neither of them actually like being called 'Dad'. Go figure! They say it's better than the confusion of me calling them both the same thing. I think they just couldn't decide when I was little which one of them should be 'Dad'. So, instead, I've got Pappy and Dada.

Pappy is brilliant at helping me with maths and we both love reading stories. Sherlock Holmes is our favourite. Pappy also knows how to braid my hair properly – which is slightly surprising, seeing as he doesn't have any hair of his own! He's a bit more serious, though. He says it's because he gets stressed by his work.

The funny one is Dada – or, as he says because of his magic, Da-Daaa! Cheesy, I know. Dada is a really good magician but he thinks he's a comedian, too. He says he just hasn't become famous yet. He knows everything there is to know about magic and yet he's so forgetful. He can remember which card you've picked from a deck of fifty-two, but never knows where he's put his own keys.

"Dems, come on! I'm just looking for my hat and then we can go."

His hat will be on a hook under a coat in the cupboard, I'm sure.

I don't have a mum, in case you were wondering. Well, not a mum who's around in my normal life, anyway. I get a birthday and Christmas

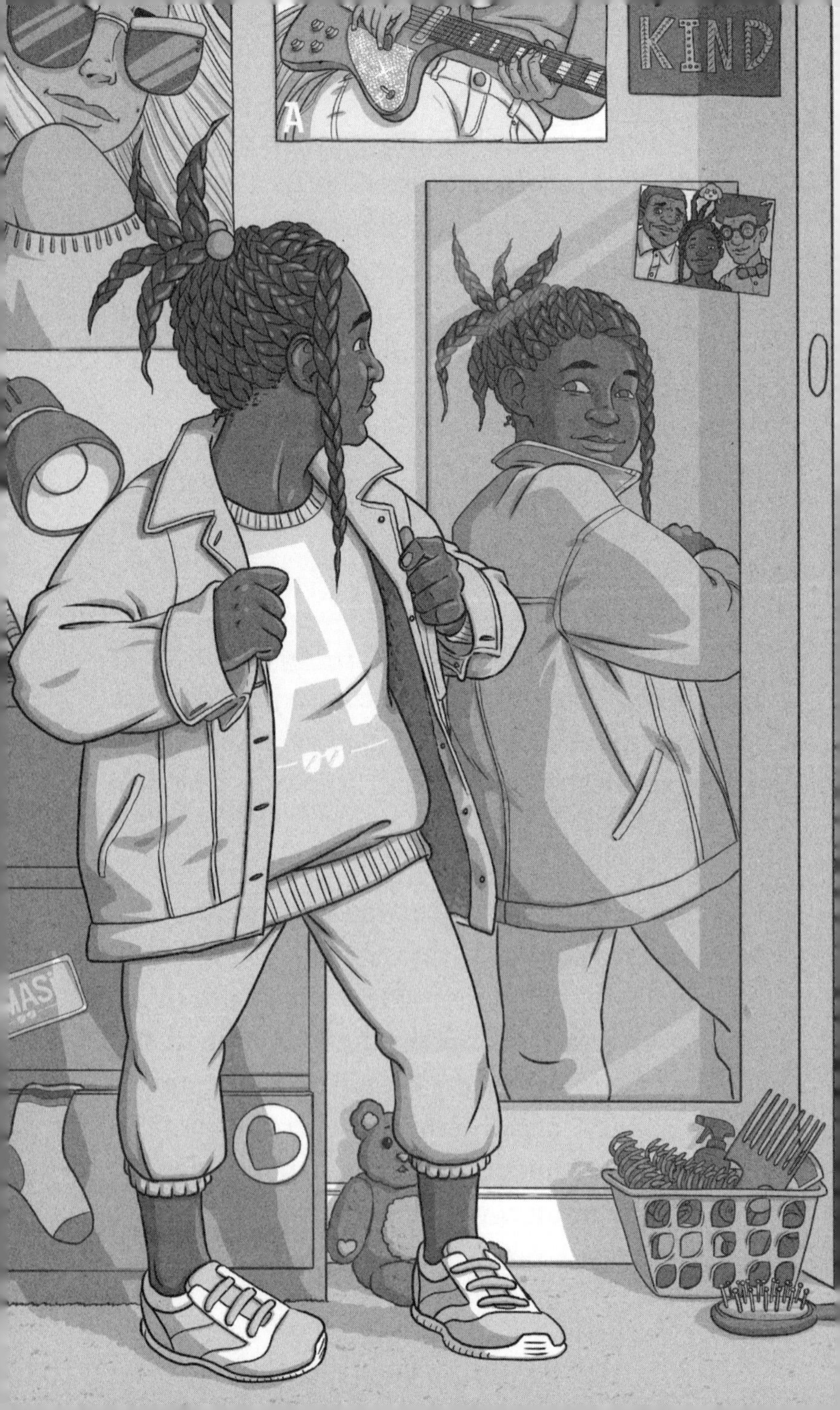
KIND

card from my actual mum, and we get on fine and stuff. She's just more like a mysterious great-aunt who you're related to but don't see all that often. Great-Aunt Mum.

"Never mind – found the hat! You coming, Dems?"

"Yeah, Dada. On my way!" I grab my denim jacket. I'm ready but I'm still bubbling over with so much excitement that it makes me dizzy. I grab a lip balm but then put it back so it's one less thing to carry. I'm ready but I still feel frantic. I try on my denim jacket instead of the puffer coat that I had previously picked out. I'm checking myself in the mirror, trying to decide for the twentieth time.

Dada is taking me into the city centre this morning, so we're catching the tram. The actual concert is not until tonight but Amasi is doing a live 'Q and A' session to launch her tour. The rumours are that it might even include a sneak-preview performance of her new single. It starts at twelve. Some lucky person won a radio competition to actually go on stage with her during the launch, too. I tried entering so many times. I wish it could have been me.

We know there'll be big crowds of people there to see her. Half of Sheffield loves her, now that she's really famous. I've been a fan for years, though. I liked her songs when she first started. Now, I know all the lyrics and sing them at the top of my voice in the shower. I watch all her vlog posts. She's so glamorous all the time – perfect hair, perfect make-up, perfect voice.

She once played a gig in this little place on the edge of the city when I was only about seven. She wasn't even called Amasi then. She was just plain Amalie Simpkins and only started calling herself Amasi later on. Dad knew this guy who was a sound engineer – he was helping her out so we went to watch. I was the only little kid there. I've been a fan ever since.

I still liked her songs when she got into a duo shortly after that but it didn't work out. She then went solo and had this massive hit called 'Follow Your Dreams', which got millions of downloads. From then on, she got more and more famous and had an even bigger success with a song called 'Steel Yourself', which was number one in the charts in loads of countries.

Now, instead of performing in a little back room with about seventeen people watching, she's got more than six million followers on her social media – that's more people than there are living in the whole of Yorkshire! She doesn't live here any more, though.

She's got this amazing house in Los Angeles – that's in the USA. She bought it when 'Steel Yourself' became a huge hit there. I've just been watching one of the videos that she shared a few weeks ago after moving in. I've watched it every day since she posted it. Everything is bursting with colour and Amasi spins around with the camera looking so happy. One wall behind her is virtually all huge glass windows and you can see nothing but bright blue sea through every one of them. Inside, there's a huge spiral staircase that leads to an enormous hallway. Outside, she's got a swimming pool and palm trees in her back garden. I imagine myself floating on an inflatable lounger in the pool, drinking something bright orange from a glass with a little umbrella in it.

I blink myself back from my imaginary trip to LA and see myself looking back from the mirror.

I decide to stick with the denim jacket.

Ready.

I rattle down our narrow stairs which lead straight into the lounge, feeling the banister wobble an inch as I hold on to it.

"Slow down, kiddo!" says Pappy as I spin off the bottom step where the carpet is the most frayed. He grabs me for a hug before heading up the stairs.

Dada is beside the front door, straightening his hat in the mirror. "You're always going a million miles per hour! Take a breath!"

"I'm just excited!" I shout and he laughs as he shakes his head.

"Actually, in case I forget, check this out before we go, Dems," suggests Dada. He points at the battered computer in the corner of the living room. It's where he's always watching videos of new magic tricks and ideas.

"What is it?" I ask. "Don't we need to go?"

"Won't take a minute. I watched this new behind-the-scenes clip last night from one of those magicians' secrets programmes. You'll love it," he tells me.

He's right – I will. I always love it when we watch magic secrets together and he talks me through ideas for the tricks he's going to try in his next act. Just when I thought we were finally going out the door, though...

This one shows the audience watching a glamorous assistant getting into something that looks like a fancy wardrobe. The whole thing spins round three hundred and sixty degrees and then the screen lights up with a blinding flash, followed by billowing smoke. When it clears, there's just the hollow frame of the wardrobe still standing. The front, back and sides have all been flipped open like a collapsing gift box and there's no sign of the assistant. Instead, she appears from behind the magician with a flourish. However, the video continues and, at first, seems to replay what we've just watched. This time, though, it pans around and shows that the assistant stepped into the wardrobe and straight out of a secret back door once the wardrobe door was closed.

"That's clever," I nod.

"Thought you'd like it," Dada beams back at me. "Might have to try and make me one of those. Come on, then. Let's get a move on."

"Have fun!" Pappy shouts to us from upstairs.

"See you later," Dada calls back to him. "Be careful!"

Pappy isn't coming with us but he's going to be working in the city centre so we might see him. He's a police officer and he has to be there because of the expected crowds. Right now, he's 'Pappy' but in an hour, he'll be on duty and he'll be 'Police Constable Akpan'. I like that Dada always tells him to be careful even though he's a grown man. It's cute.

Chapter Two

We take the tram and it's already busier than it normally is on a Saturday. Dada and I sit opposite each other and he keeps pulling a deliberately goofy face to make me smile. I look around at everyone and wonder where they're going, hoping they don't catch me looking at them.

Sometimes, we play the lookalike game. If we see someone who's a lookalike of somebody famous, then we point them out to each other. As I glance from face to face on the tram, I wonder who else might be going to Amasi's tour launch and if they've ever seen her perform before. Better still, I imagine where else they might be going. I also like to play this game in my head. Sometimes, I try to work out the right answer just as Sherlock Holmes would do, from clues like things that they're wearing or carrying; sometimes, I just like to imagine the wildest answers I can.

On the other side of the aisle, two girls are fidgeting on either side of their mother. They are younger than me – they look about six and nine. The older one is wearing an Amasi T-shirt. The younger one has big, pink, plastic sunglasses just like Amasi wears on stage. No prizes for guessing that they're probably going to the launch, too.

Farther away than them is a lady on her own. On the seat next to her, she has a cardboard box overflowing with packs of sandwiches. My brow creases as I imagine where she's going. Maybe she's going to give them all out to people who are homeless or maybe she's just on the way home with them to prepare for a party. Instead, I imagine she's trying to break the world record for a house made of sandwiches. These packs will be the finishing touches to complete her roof. The creases smooth out from my brow and the corners of my mouth turn up with the picture in my head.

Behind Dada are a couple of older boys, maybe sixteen or seventeen. Even boys their age like Amasi, whether they admit to it or not. I can't tell if they're going to the launch event, though. Nothing gives them away. They're just loud and messy with their fast-food paper bags and drinks. An old lady in a hat, farther down the carriage, tuts at them.

"See the old lady?" I whisper to Dada. He looks over his shoulder to follow my line of sight.

"With the blue handbag and matching hat?" he checks.

"Yeah. Lookalike of The Queen," I say.

He looks again and then snorts out a laugh. "Good one," he nods. I smile at being able to make him laugh.

I notice that behind the young girls and their mum, there's someone sitting in a single seat.

A man, I think – but I'm not sure as he has his baseball cap pulled down low over his eyes. It says 'California' across the front, which is not something that you see in Sheffield every day. It's not a cold morning but he has a brown, woollen jacket on with the collar turned up. Mirrored sunglasses, too, though not pink ones like Amasi wears. I look away because I can't tell whether he's looking back at me or not.

"Hey – isn't that your friend from school?" Dada says, a little too loudly. He points down into the middle section of the tram. My heart takes a dive towards my stomach.

"Oh. Um, yeah. That's Celeste. She's in my class but she's not really a friend," I reply.

'Not really a friend'. That's an understatement. Not a friend at *all*. She told me that I was immature for liking Amasi. She thinks she's great because she gets to go to places like the city centre with her older sister and her sister's friends – just as she is now. She says I'm just a kid because I'm only allowed if I'm with Dada or Pappy.

"Maybe she's coming to the launch, too. Want to say hi?"

"No, thanks." I try to brush off Dada's suggestion without giving him reason to ask more about her. Why would she be going into Sheffield today, anyway? She's looking towards us and I'm not sure whether she sees me or not, but I'm certain she scowls.

"OK. Well, do you know those other girls she's with?" He nods in their general direction. "They could be a girl band. They're lookalikes of the Spice Girls."

"What? Aren't the Spice Girls a bit old?" I say.

"Well, I mean when the Spice Girls were younger, not like they are now!" he replies. It distracts me from wondering whether Celeste was giving me a mean look or not. We giggle again.

"The next stop by request will be: Cathedral," comes the announcement.

"That's us!" I grin.

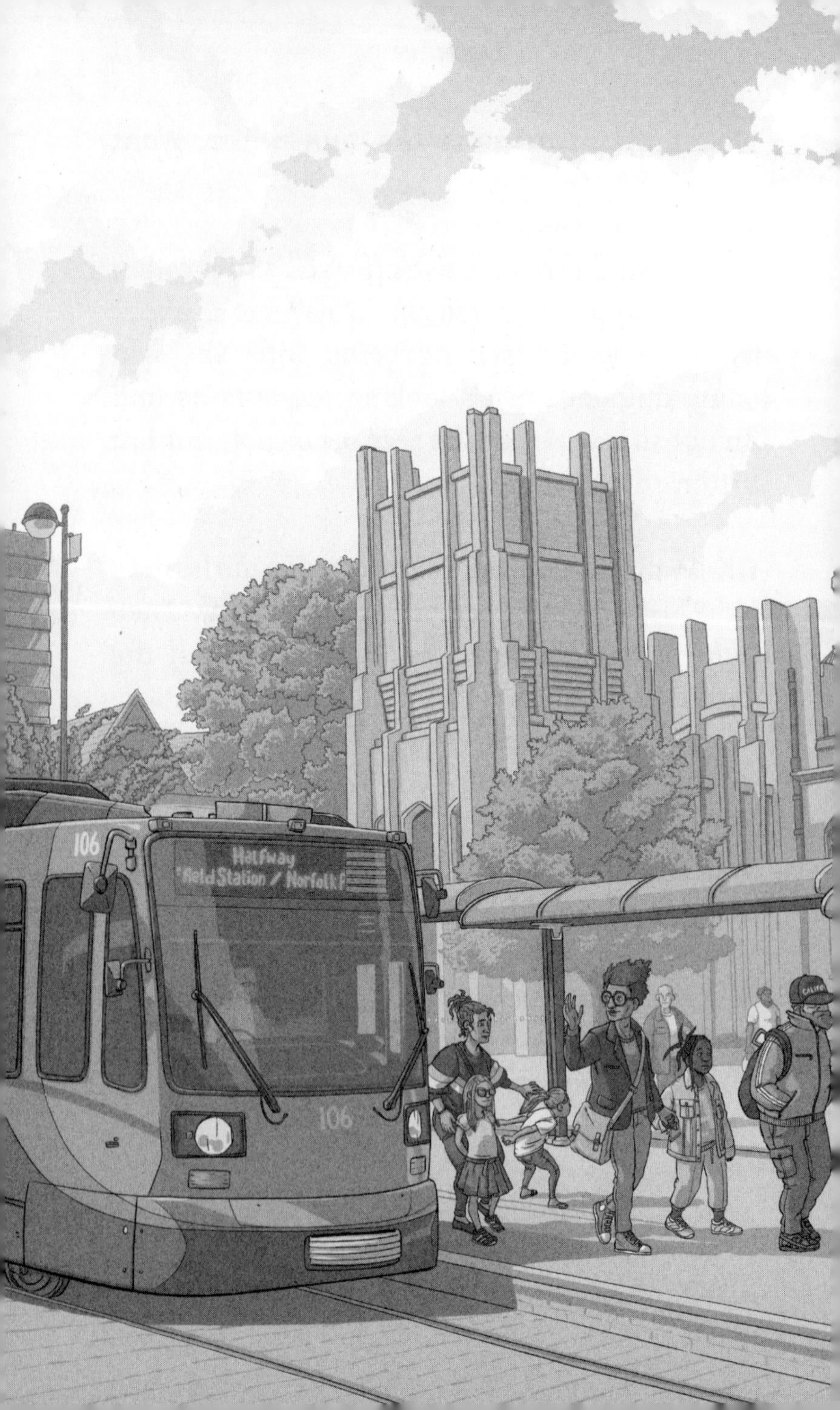

106
Halfway
106

We get off the tram near the huge cathedral and cross the road to walk up Fargate. The paving setts make a pretty pattern of curves under our feet. There are no cars – it's for people only, with trees and benches down the middle. Stepping from toe to toe, I try to keep my trainers in contact with only the bricks and not the lines between them. I pretend that if I step on a crack, the bricks will open up and swallow me whole.

I keep this up until I nearly bump into an old lady pulling along a shopping trolley and Dada tells me to look where I'm going. I look up and see lots more Amasi T-shirts and kids wearing oversized sunglasses. This event is going to be so cool!

The buildings are really tall on either side of us here, putting half of the street in shadow and half in sunlight. Shops are on the ground floor but there are three or four rows of windows rising above. In front of the shops are some little pop-up stalls with people selling merchandise: flags with Amasi's face on, whistles, lanyards, posters... It's not even nine in the morning but it feels like the start of a carnival. The atmosphere is buzzing. Dada points out two teenage girls singing along to 'Steel Yourself' and then I spot a boy who looks around five eating a cloud of candyfloss about as big as his head!

"Look at the size of that! Can I have some?" I exclaim to Dada.

"Not right now. Let's save the pennies for something later," he smiles back at me.

The smell of it wafts along behind the boy, teasing my nostrils. My stomach froths like an ocean wave, either from the candyfloss making me hungry or, more likely, the giddiness at the thought of seeing Amasi live in just a matter of hours! I take a deep breath. I absolutely, totally cannot wait!

Chapter Three

We circle around Sheffield Town Hall as we mingle with the crowds. It's an amazing Victorian building, built over a hundred years ago. Even on a normal day, the wide streets surrounding it are the busiest in the city centre. One side of the town hall looks over the Peace Gardens: a beautiful seating area with stone steps, patches of grass and fountains that shoot water straight out of the ground. Today, we can see a stage set up with huge screens and speakers on either side.

"Remember when I would run through those water fountains when I was little?" I ask Dada.

"Yeah, of course – every summer holiday. I'd chase you through them for fun. You'd get soaking wet but you'd laugh the whole time and then shake yourself off like a dog and make everyone else wet!"

"And then Pappy would wrap the big, green towel around me and we would go for ice creams at Giuseppe and Benito's cafe," I say.

Dada smiles at the memory and gives my hand a squeeze as we stroll on. "You're growing up way too fast for my liking!" he tells me.

Round the corner of the town hall are the front steps leading down to Pinstone Street. The other side of the building is farther round and borders Surrey Street. I know the area from all the times we've caught the tram to the city centre on weekends and holidays.

I tend to notice signs and street names. I don't know why. Pappy says I'd make a good police detective because I'm observant. I think that's what he wants me to be when I grow up. Dada says I'd be a better magician because I'm inquisitive and can work things out but I also

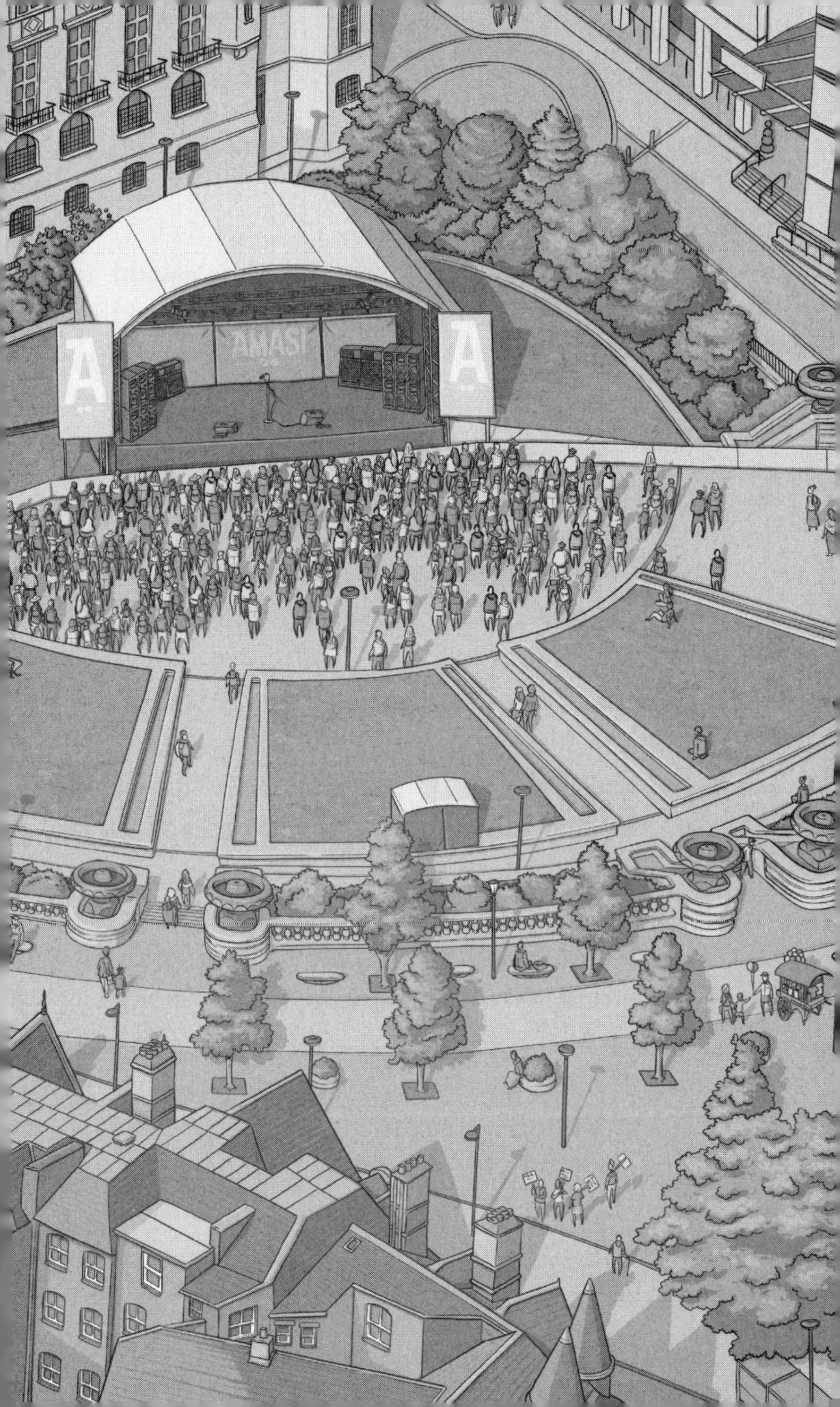
A
AMASI
A

know how to be sneaky! I can't decide which I'd prefer.

I get out my phone to take photos. I want to remember absolutely everything about this day. I hold it in front of me and tap to get pictures of the stage, the flags and the groups of excited people. We circle round twice, just taking it all in.

There are more flag sellers at the edge of the Peace Gardens. One has a huge trolley as a portable stand, full of brightly coloured souvenirs. It's a cart on wheels and it's so big that you could climb inside it for a ride. I imagine one of the loud boys from the tram getting inside and the other pushing him down a steep hill. A man stands behind the cart wearing a sample of each item: a huge hat with bells jingling, a whistle around his neck, colourful wristbands and an Amasi T-shirt over his normal clothes.

I take a photo of the seller as he smiles at me and wafts his arm across his cart to present all his items. "Come and get your flags, T-shirts, posters," he roars and then dips a bubble wand into a tub of liquid and sends huge bubbles soaring into the air.

My eyes follow the bubbles up to the clear, blue sky. Dada puts his hand on my back to guide me sideways as I nearly bump into a small crowd of people. When I see them properly, I notice that they are all holding up placards on wooden poles.

"What are they doing?" I ask.

"Some kind of protest, I think," Dada answers but we skirt around the group. I look back over my shoulder and see them bobbing their placards up and down. Painted letters say things like 'Stop the Tour – Save the World!' and 'Peace Not Pop Stars'.

"Don't they want the concert to happen?"

"I don't know." Dada ushers me along. "I wouldn't worry about them."

A couple of them smile at me warmly. I spot the lady from the tram with the sandwiches, handing some of them out. She gives one pack to a man with a huge mane of shaggy, blonde hair. His crafty eyes meet mine as I'm looking over my shoulder and he waves a leaflet at me. I only manage a quick glimpse of the headline on it: 'Costly Tours Kill Our Environment'. Underneath, there is something about how much carbon dioxide is created by planes and buses. I'm not able to read it all, though, before Dada grasps my hand and whisks me away through the crowds.

I look where we're going and when I glance back, the man with the shaggy mane is no longer looking at us; he's forcing leaflets into the hands of passers-by whether they want one or not. I'm glad to leave the protesters behind and head back to the top of Fargate. I like watching people and some of them seemed nice but I didn't like the look of him. Something about him gave me the creeps.

We see people in pairs, wearing matching orange hi-vis jackets which say 'Event Steward' in bold letters. I see a couple of police officers, too, with their crackling radios attached near their shoulders. Pappy is not on duty yet, though. There's a busker on the corner of Surrey Street, sitting cross-legged on the floor playing a guitar. He's wearing a black jacket and has his hood over his head. He plays a gentle, sad song. I realise that it's actually one of Amasi's songs but it's different. It's a really slow version of 'Follow Your Dreams'. Dada gives me a couple of coins to throw into the busker's collection. Between lines of his song, he glances up, nods and says, "Thanks, flower." I want to tell him to play something happier and then he might get more money but we're past him before there's a chance.

Another woman, who we hear before we see, comes striding past us with her short hair brushed into a big quiff at the front. She's wearing a tight pair of jeans and shiny, black shoes. She's in a white, blazer-type jacket with a black collar but it's pinned down by the straps of a giant rucksack on her back that would be large enough for all her belongings if she were going camping for a whole week.

We hear her because, at the front of each rucksack strap, in the same kind of place that the police officers have their radios, she has attached a mini speaker so that music blasts from each side of her chest. It's not an Amasi song that's playing, though; it's something with a fast, thudding beat that has turned her into a walking disco. Dada and I look at each other as the woman passes, dancing as she moves. Dada does an embarrassing little dance as she goes by and then we both laugh at the same time.

"All kinds of people here today, Dems. Lookalike of Elvis Presley, she was!"

"Never heard of him," I say. Dada gives me a wide-eyed look.

We spend a little more time wandering through the crowds, soaking up the atmosphere. An announcement is made from the huge speakers at the side of the stage, saying that Amasi's tour bus is running late because of a diversion.

The protesters cheer at this announcement.

"Never mind diverting it. Stop it altogether!" one of them shouts. I think it came from the man with the shaggy, blonde hair.

"Why are they being so mean?" I ask.

"I don't think they're trying to be mean," Dada says. "I just think they care about the environment."

"Well don't they even know how much Amasi cares for the environment, too? Everyone going to the concert can use the bus or tram for free with their show ticket, just like we did. Plus, she's spoken loads about making the tour bus eco-friendly and getting rid of plastic waste at the concerts," I point out.

"Well that's all pretty impressive. Maybe they don't realise those things," Dada replied.

I spot that man again from the tram with the sunglasses and baseball cap. He doesn't look like he'd be an Amasi fan. He's hanging around near the stage, though. I think he looks a bit suspicious. I try to remember whether he showed the tram conductor a show ticket too, or if he paid like normal.

I wonder what Amasi is doing now. Is she getting ready on the bus? What would she think about the protest? Is she having a nap while travelling in? I'd love to perform on a huge stage just like her one day but I think I'd want to do a mixture of singing and magic. I wouldn't get to do that if I became a detective, though.

"I wonder if Amasi gets nervous still?" I ask Dada. I think about how nervous I get when I have to go to the front of the whole school in assembly. My legs wobble and my head feels heavy.

"Probably," he replies. "There's nothing wrong with a few nerves before going on stage. It shows that you care and that it's important to you."

"She's superstitious, you know," I tell him, even though I've told him these things before. I tell him again because he's probably forgotten. "I've read about some of the things she always does before a concert. Do you know, she always wears the same silver boots? Not just the same type but the same actual pair – has done for years. Plus, she always calls her nanna and grandad before going on stage to thank them for all they did when they were bringing her up."

"That's sweet. Are you going to call me and Pappy before every gig if you become famous?" Dada asks with a smile.

"We'll see!" I reply. "And, of course, what most people know is that she always has to have her iconic guitar. She says she couldn't play without it. It's like a lucky charm but it's also perfectly tuned for her."

"Ah, the famous guitar. Yep, even I know about that."

"It's been customised and it's got these expensive diamonds on, now. I read that it might be worth thousands or even millions of pounds, now that she's so famous!"

"That sure is some instrument, then," Dada says but he's looking over the heads of the crowd and distracted by a commotion. Something is happening among the crowd. Something is getting out of hand.

Chapter Four

There is some pushing and shoving not far from us. I see a flash of orange from a couple of the event stewards and even a police officer. They are surrounded by other people in the crowd, which is now much bigger than it was two hours ago. Among it all, one of the placards from a protester pokes up above everyone's heads, bobbing around like it's in the sea.

It's a large, open section of the city centre where Fargate meets Surrey Street and a few other roads. The town hall is on one corner with shops and huge buildings on opposite sides. Even on regular days, Fargate is for pedestrians only.

There are benches and trees down the middle of the road but no cars. Some people stand on the benches for a better view of what is going on. All heads turn to check out the disturbance.

"Looks like the protest is getting a bit out of hand," Dada says.

I can hear a mixture of cheering and booing. I can see the crowd jostling but I can't tell what's going on. I pull my phone from my pocket again to get pictures. The man with the shaggy, blonde hair is there.

"Can I go on your shoulders?" I ask.

"Thought you were too big for that now?" Dada raises an eyebrow at me. He lifts me anyway, taking off his hat first, and I peer over the heads to get a better look, holding the phone camera out in front of me.

"Get him outta here!" someone shouts from off to our right. I turn my head to look. Beneath me, Dada takes a step to steady himself. The crowds have grown much more and there are people behind us now as well as to both sides of us.

We're not squashed but the gaps are shrinking.

"Move aside please... Excuse me... Make some room, please..." Two more police officers appear from somewhere to our left. They push urgently through the mingling onlookers. Up ahead, the placard with 'Peace Not Pop Stars' bobs up one more time and then is sucked down into the crowd.

"What's happening?" Dada calls up to me.

"I think one of those protesters is going to be taken away by the police," I tell Dada, looking down. "He's making a real fuss."

"I guess some fans have got frustrated with them," Dada suggests, but I'm not so sure.

"I don't think it's that," I say. "It looks like it's the other protesters who are shouting at him. I don't think he's one of them."

"Oh, well. Think you're ready to come back down now, then? You're getting pretty heavy, you know!"

"Just two more minutes, Dada," I plead. I'm nosy and want to get a better look at the person being led through the crowd and who is now heading towards us. I pull out my phone and zoom in on him using the camera feature. It's not the man with the mane of shaggy, blonde hair; it's a different protester. He's not shouting about the environment but I can't tell properly what he's saying.

He's wearing a baggy, green jacket. The fur around his hood hangs over his head and obscures his face. His hands are handcuffed together in front of him. I snap a couple of photos and feel like a reporter. There's a police officer on either side of him, one holding on to his arms and the other clearing a path through the crowd. As he gets closer, I see he has a huge bag on his back, like the ones that fit about fifteen netballs in at school. That's weird. It's the second person today carrying such a massive bag. I see why, though – his placards have been stuffed into it and the wooden poles stick out of the top like two fence posts making a letter 'V' behind his head.

"Keep music real!" he shouts loudly. "We don't

need Amasi. We want proper music!"

He doesn't seem so bothered about the environment; it's more like he's got a particular issue with Amasi. Now that *is* just mean.

They are quite near to us when one of the police officers presses her radio. "Emergency plan: Golf Papa Bravo," she says into it, with a voice that sounds like my teacher in a bad mood.

The radio crackles with a reply which I can't make out properly.

"Roger that," she says into the radio and then turns to the other police officer to instruct him.

"The bus is arriving around the back instead and they need extra bodies there. You go. I'll take him from here and get him in the box."

"All right, if you're sure," her partner replies.

"No problem. Get this lot dispersed as you go and clear this street."

I'm still being nosy and now I'm even more

intrigued but Dada calls up to me again. He can't move his head much with me in the way. I'm looking down onto his hair, which is thick like a bird's nest. I bet I could rummage around in it and find a twig or two. Actually, a rabbit or a dove would be more likely, knowing Dada.

"Demi, you're gonna have to come down now. My shoulders are about to give way!"

"Oh, please, one more minute. I just want to see what happens!" I plead. My attention is back on the drama that is unfolding. A surge of people begins to build around us.

The two police officers have separated. The woman is holding on to the protester at the corner of Surrey Street. The male officer is making his way down the street with his arms out wide, like he's herding sheep. He has gone past a red telephone box and a few parked cars but the gap between them is now empty of pedestrians.

"PC Mullins – radio if you need me!" he calls back to her.

"I'll be fine," she says, keeping a firm grip as the protester squirms and pulls his arm.

Chapter Five

The police officer frogmarches the protester to the old, green police box which is well known by all of Sheffield. The green, wooden structure is no bigger than a pair of phone boxes joined together. It looks a bit like a tiny garden shed. The back of the box is pushed up against one wall of the town hall. The front has a sign at the top which says 'South Yorkshire Police'. We pass by it all the time and I've looked it up on the Internet before.

There used to be a few similar boxes in the country that the police used, before police cars were common or mobile phones were invented.

They could be used to phone back to the station. They could also be used for temporarily locking up a suspect until they were transported away.

"Dada, I think they're putting him into the police box," I say.

"All right, well the show's over then. You're definitely coming down now. I think I'm an inch shorter than when you went up there." He lifts me over his head and lowers me in front of him until my feet touch the ground again. As he rubs at his shoulders, I complain because I'm missing the last bit of the excitement. Instead, I peer through the bodies and try to glimpse the end of the drama.

"Look! They really are. Remember, Pappy said that it might be used if needed in an emergency. It will be the first time in over fifty years, he told us."

"Oh, yeah. I do remember him talking about it. Are you sure they're locking someone up in it?" Dada asks and starts craning his neck to look over in the same direction as me.

I see the police officer – PC Mullins, the other officer called her – unlock the door to the box. People keep getting in the way but I manoeuvre my head between the bodies and watch her pull open the door. She bundles the protester into the open doorway but then there's some kind of scuffle.

"Uh-oh," I gulp as I try to keep my eyes on the scene. It looks like she's scrabbling to get the man into the box. He's out of sight behind the open door. She looks like she's pushing at him and then she staggers back. She recovers her footing and pushes again with one hand while the other is on the door trying to close it. Eventually, she scrambles the door shut and leans her back against it. Beneath her black padded vest, her underlayer has become untucked and her hat has ended upside down on the ground. Even from a distance, I see her chest rise and fall with big, deep breaths.

"What happened?" Dada asks.

"I think she had some trouble getting him in there," I tell him. "Looks like she's finally managed now, though. That was a bit scary."

"Don't worry, Dems," he says. "If that man was up to no good, then at least it's sorted out now. Looks like the real action is going to be happening soon!" He points past the town hall steps to the crowds now moving towards the top of the Peace Gardens.

40

"Looks like everyone is heading to where they can see the stage. If the bus has arrived, then the show could be starting any time. Come on!" I urge him.

We follow the crowd moving along Pinstone Street to where we'll be able to look down into the Peace Gardens. The speakers from the sides of the stage crackle back into life. Another announcement is being made.

"Ladies and gentlemen, boys and girls. We are very sorry for the delay. The tour bus had to take an unexpected detour but I now have great news!" The crowd cheers, even though the news hasn't been announced yet. Any noise from the remaining protesters is drowned out. "The star you have all been waiting for has just arrived!"

An even bigger cheer goes up. My heart quickens and thumps inside my chest like it's trying to get out. I stand on my tiptoes. I can just about see the tiny man on the stage speaking into the microphone. He raises his voice as he goes on.

"The bus has arrived just this minute on the street behind me. I can tell you that Amasi will be live on this stage for her Q and A in only a few more moments. Are you all ready?"

The biggest cheer of all rises from the crowd in response to his question. I can't keep still. I dance from toe to toe and cling on to Dada's sleeve.

A few minutes pass as we watch people dash onto the stage one by one and fiddle with wires and microphones and a drum kit. One wiry man with a scruffy beard and long, grey hair in a ponytail taps on the microphone in the centre of the stage. The sound of his taps is echoed and amplified through the speakers. He's wearing a faded, black T-shirt with a bunch of beads wrapped around his wrist and more dangling around his neck. On the T-shirt is a picture of a big pair of red lips with a tongue sticking out. He puts a bottle of water down next to the microphone and then walks away.

Another couple of minutes later, he walks back carrying a gleaming purple guitar case and places it down near the water. For a moment, he stops and stares out at the crowd. Even though it's daylight, there are bright spotlights shining on him. I see him put his hand to his forehead like a salute as he scans around from side to side. He twirls the beads around his finger and strokes his beard. Then, he slopes off again.

The spotlights go off and the background music that has been playing fades away. My heart feels like it's being beaten by the drummer in the backing band. The screens at the side of the stage go blank and there's a hush.

Chapter Six

"I think Amasi's coming on," Dada says. "Do you want to come back up? My shoulders might just have recovered."

I grin as he heaves me back up onto his shoulders. There's an electric kind of buzz flickering through the crowd, now. Flags are waving and some people shout Amasi's name. Dada is holding on to my legs so I reach my arms high into the air.

Just as I do, I see her. Amasi is striding up to the steps at the side of the stage: perfect hair in a high ponytail tumbling down her back; huge, pink sunglasses; the coolest outfit. Sometimes, I imagine what it would be like if she were my big sister. Without even meaning to, I let out a happy squeal.

After Amasi reaches the microphone stand in the centre of the stage, the crowd just keeps on cheering and chanting. Her face is enlarged a hundred times on the screens on either side of the stage where she stands. She waits a while with a huge smile on her face, looking around. Then, she motions with her arms for everyone to bring down the noise.

"Hello, Sheffield!" she bellows into the microphone. The crowd go wild again. "It's so good to be back here in my home city! Are you all having fun already?"

I know she can't hear me but I scream as loud as my lungs will allow me. "Yeeeaah!"

"You guys are all coming to the concert tonight, I hope?" she says.

"Yeah!" the crowd roars back as one. I bet not all of them are. The tickets were really expensive

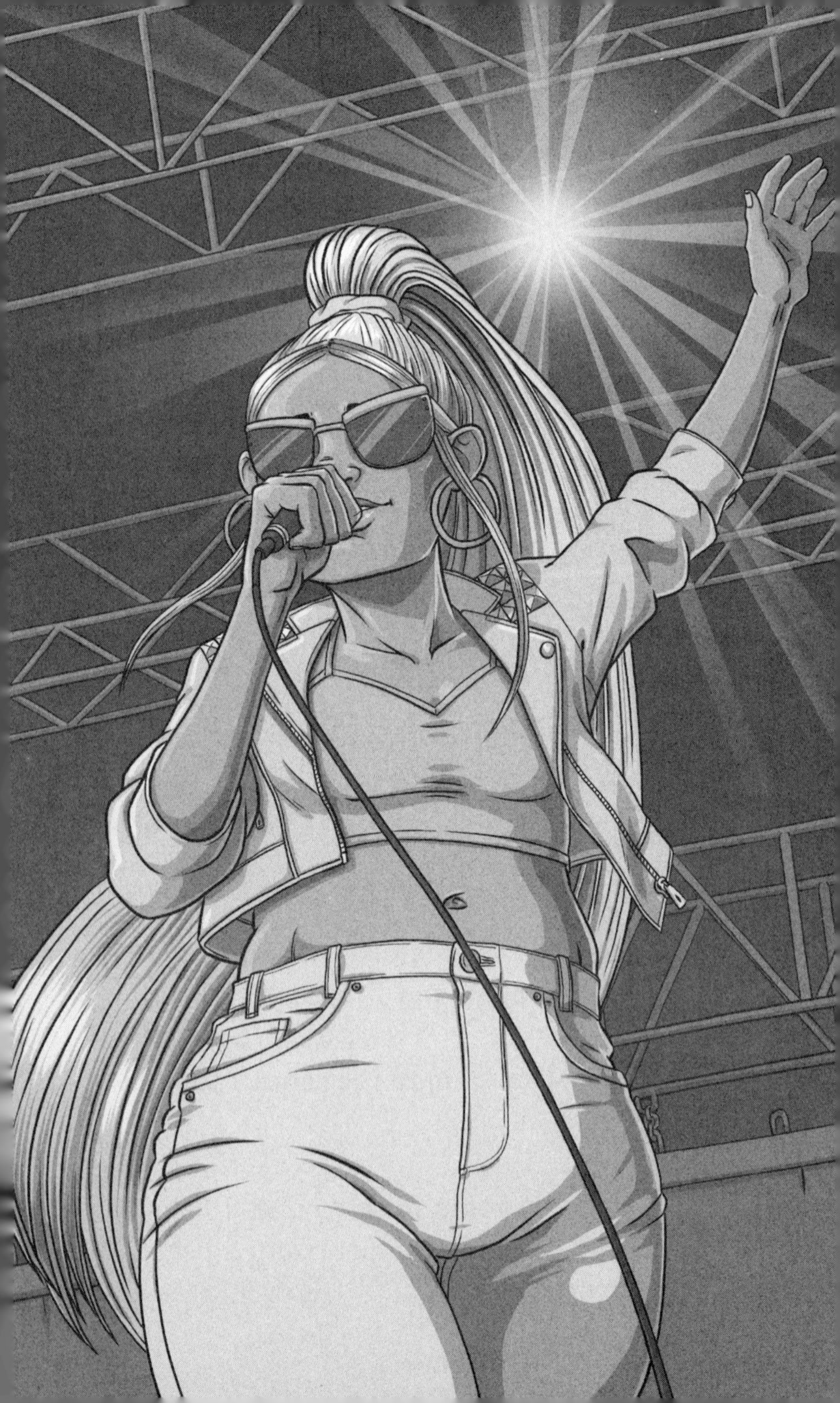

and sold out within minutes. Pappy said it might have to be a combined birthday and Christmas present for me but I didn't mind. I even emptied my savings tin into Pappy's hands to show how much I wanted to go.

"Do you guys wanna hear a quick song now to get us in the mood?" Amasi asks.

"Yeah!" everyone roars back again.

Amasi is laughing as she takes a swig from her water bottle and then leans over to open the guitar case. She crouches and flicks open the two catches. She carefully flips up the lid of the case.

No guitar.

We can all see that the case is empty apart from a rotten lump of wood. On the big screens, the camera zooms in on it, sitting among the silk, purple lining inside.

"What... where..." Her questions don't form properly.

At first, Amasi looks across to the people at the side of the stage and she is still smiling, like maybe it's a joke. The big screens switch to a shot of her face again. I watch the corners of her mouth draw away from her cheeks, her brow creasing.

"Where is it?" she asks and stands up, directing the words to someone off the edge of the stage. She is still right next to the microphone, though, and her question is broadcast for us all, tainted with a tone of concern. She puts her hand over the microphone and asks again, "Where's the guitar?"

Although her voice is muffled, we can all still hear. Amasi's face has changed now from confusion to concern. Her words are more urgent. The guitar is missing. *The* guitar. The ponytailed guy jogs across the stage and looks at the empty guitar case as if to confirm it definitely does not contain a guitar. He strokes his beard again. A high-pitched noise zips from the speakers followed by a crackle. The sound has been cut now because Amasi is still speaking and waving her arms around but it's not coming through the speakers.

We're all watching. Murmurs start to come from the crowd.

Another high-pitched screech sounds, which makes me clasp my hands over my ears for a moment. Then, Amasi's voice is back through the speakers, although she obviously doesn't mean for it to be. She is still facing the guy in the black T-shirt with the red lips logo.

"What do you mean, 'gone'? I can see that it's gone! *Where* has it gone?"

"It was in there when we unloaded from the bus. I've just carried it up here. No one else has been near it," he replies, shrugging his shoulders and twiddling the beads around his neck.

The crowd is now silent and watching this play out on stage. I can feel a knot in my tummy. I feel upset for her. She will be devastated.

"That guitar is my life. It is priceless! I can't play without it. You know how important it is to me, Nick. How can it have just disappeared if it was in the case when I left the bus and, now, it's not there? I need that guitar back or there's no way I can perform tonight!"

The crowd lets out a collective gasp. At this point, a smartly dressed woman strides across from the other side of the stage. When she reaches the guitar case, she spots something inside it that no one else seems to have noticed. Attached to the piece of wood is some paper, tied with string. She reaches down and pulls off the scrap of paper. As she reads it, her mouth drops open a touch and she puts her hand on Amasi's shoulder and then speaks into the microphone.

"I'm really sorry, ladies and gentlemen. It appears we have a bit of a problem," she says, looking out at the crowd. She then turns her head to address someone else back where she came from. At the same time, she makes this gesture of slicing one finger across her neck. "Cut the sound, please, Tim."

Whoever Tim is, he's not quick enough because Amasi reads the note out loud as it's shown to her. The words hit me like a smack in the face.

"What's that supposed to mean?" she asks. "Keep music real."

Chapter Seven

Without speaking, Dada crouches down and lifts me over his head to place me back on the ground. My legs feel like jelly and they don't quite support me as I stand. I'm not sure whether it's because they were in an awkward position on Dada's shoulders, or something else. I reach out and hold on to him as he straightens back up.

The words from the scrap of paper are still ringing in my ears. "What's going to happen?" I ask.

I can tell he doesn't have the answer.

On stage, Amasi has fallen to her knees and I think she is crying. She has the scrap of paper in her hand. The smartly dressed woman is comforting her and Nick with the ponytail has his hands on his head. Two police officers appear on stage next and they all gather around Amasi. Eventually, they guide her to her feet and then off the side of the stage.

"Let's see if we can get round the back of the town hall and see what's going on," I say to Dada.

"I doubt we'll get anywhere near the stage or the bus, if that's what you're thinking," he replies, shaking his head.

"Pleeeeease," I beg. "We can try!"

Dada grins, rolls his eyes and grabs my hand as he turns. He likes an adventure just as much as I do. We start weaving our way through the mumbling crowd. An announcement comes over the speakers as we're leaving.

"Ladies and gentlemen, I'm sorry but this event is, unfortunately, being postponed. We'll update you as soon as we..."

I don't catch the last bit. We're dashing back along Pinstone Street, past the town hall steps and round the corner to Surrey Street. As we do, I see two more police officers running towards us. My breath catches in my throat for a moment as it seems as if they're coming straight towards me. Instead, they stop at the green police box.

"Dada, wait!" I say, sensing we might catch some of the excitement here. The words on the scrap of paper come back to me.

"Remember what Amasi just read on that note? 'Keep music real'. That's what the protester said when he was being marched away."

We slow our pace and take a wide arc so that we're positioned to see straight into the green police box as one of the officers fumbles with a bunch of keys, trying to unlock the door.

"Maybe the protester is the same person that put the note in the guitar case," I say out loud. "If it's just been stolen between being taken off the bus and getting on stage, then it must have only just happened. Maybe he's escaped and has taken the guitar!"

"Escaped? Not if he was locked in from the outside," Dada points out.

"It must be him! The words on the note – that's exactly what he said!" I argue. "I bet he's not in there. He's probably got out through the window or the roof or a secret underground passageway!"

One of the police officers finally gets the right key in the lock. He pulls down on the handle and opens the door. From our angle, we see right between the two officers into the empty space of the police box.

"Look! I told you!" I point at the empty space.

Dada screws up his eyes.

Then, the protester steps into view. We didn't notice him just inside the box, his hands still cuffed together at the wrists. He's definitely still in there. He looks happy, almost smirking.

Two more officers arrive from down the road, radios babbling, and another officer runs from up the road. The last one to arrive is the female officer who wrestled the protester into the box. She has her hat back on, now. If she ever managed to smarten her black top under her vest, though, it's become untucked again now from her sprint.

They all gather around the green police box in consultation. I keep hold of Dada's hand but edge forwards to listen, dragging him a few steps closer.

I can just about see into the little, green booth. Much of the open doorway is now filled by the shape of the protester. I didn't catch much of a glimpse earlier when he was being marched away, but now that I can see him, his face is oddly familiar. His bag of placards is strapped to his back with the sign part of the placards down inside the bag. The two posts are sticking out upside down behind his shoulders. Higher up than the posts reach, there are some coat hooks on the wall behind him.

There's a group of five police officers – joined by two event stewards in their hi-vis jackets – now huddled around. PC Mullins, who managed to get him into the box in the first place, steps inside and pats down the man's legs, checking his pockets. She feels the bag from the outside and then peers inside it before shaking her head at the other officers.

One of them turns away from the others to speak into the radio at his shoulder, tilting his head down to the left as he steps a pace or two away.

"PC Sanderson here, Sarge. Nothing to report,

I'm afraid," I can just about catch him saying. "Suspect still detained and has been searched. Securely locked inside for the last hour, exactly where PC Mullins left him. He hasn't moved, Sarge. He's in the clear." He releases his fingers from the radio button that he was holding and looks back at the others.

"I'll take him in for questioning anyway," says PC Mullins. "There's a vehicle on the way."

"All right. We'll go and join the search around Pinstone Street and surrounding roads," the officer who identified himself as PC Sanderson replies. He walks briskly away with another officer, heading up the street from where we came. Within moments, a police van pulls up on the opposite pavement between us and the green police box.

PC Mullins leads the protester from his temporary cell round to the back of the van. With his hands cuffed in front of him, there's no way of taking his huge rucksack off. She puts her hand on his head to make sure it's not bumped as he steps into the van. His bag of placards on his back follows him in. The door is slammed shut.

Chapter Eight

"I'll take it from here," PC Mullins tells the last two remaining police officers. She gets into the front passenger seat to join the driver and the van turns round to go back the way it came.

As it leaves, one of the flag sellers from earlier passes by with his big cart. He must have given up early on the merchandise sales. I feel a little smile as I see the two boys from the tram straight afterwards and remember that I pictured them pushing each other down a hill in that cart. Thankfully, they're not doing that but chasing each other around and showing off. My smile is gone as quickly as it forms, though, as I think of Amasi and how devastated she must be at the guitar being missing. I watch all her vlogs and read every article about her. That guitar means everything to her, not to mention that it's also worth a huge amount of money to everyone else.

We watch the police van as it pulls slowly away and turns left at the end of the road. The two police officers left behind stand and chat for a moment. We're on the other side of the road so I can't hear what they're saying. I pull Dada's hand and we cross over so that now they're only a few metres in front of us. I tilt my head and try to listen to their conversation.

"What d'you make of it?" says the first one.

"Still something fishy, if you ask me," replies the other.

Dada gives my arm a tug, not realising at first why I'm not moving. Then, he seems to recognise what I'm doing and purses his lips.

"Well, he couldn't have nabbed the guitar, could he? Locked in that box with the cuffs on the whole time," the first one says.

"Nah, I know. Just looked so smug, though," comes the reply as they turn to walk away.

I look up at Dada to check if he was listening, too.

"Sneaky girl. You don't miss a trick, do you?" he laughs.

"They don't know where the guitar is or who's taken it, do they?" I ask, seriously.

"Seems not, Dems. Why would someone do it?" he fires back.

"Because it's so valuable! Or because they're just jealous!" I tell him.

"Well, I suppose you're right there."

"It's not fair – what about the concert? She can't play without the guitar!"

"It's just a guitar, Dems. I'm sure they'll get her a spare or a backup or something."

"No, you don't understand. I read this interview she did online. She says that guitar feels like a part of her. That article said that her success has grown and grown ever since she started playing with it so she just wouldn't consider performing without it now. Plus, it's been customised with diamonds so it's worth loads. *Plus*, it's sentimental. Even if she could play without it, she'd be too upset that it's still missing."

"All right, fair enough. I get that it's important to her." He holds his hands up in a kind of surrender and then glances at the newsagents a few paces away. "Hey, while we're here, do you want a quick snack or something? I might go in and get a drink."

Dada looks at me, waiting for a response. I search his eyes to see whether or not he understands the importance of what I'm saying. Was he even listening properly? If I had to pick which one of my dads would be more likely to understand or go along with a plan of mine, then it would be Dada. Pappy is just a little bit more strict.

I don't want anything from the newsagents. Right now, I can feel this urge burning inside me and I know I can help find that guitar.

I have an idea, but I'm not sure whether or not to tell Dada. If I told Dada and he agreed, great. If he told me not to do it, then I would have to decide whether or not to do it anyway and risk getting into trouble. If I don't say anything first, then technically, I'm not actually disobeying him.

"No, thanks," I say. "I'll wait out here."

Dada strides over and pushes open the door of the newsagents. A bell jingles above to indicate to the owner that someone is entering. After the door closes, I count in my head.

One... two... three...

Then, I dash across the road. I've never done anything like this before. If I can just quickly get inside that box and back out again before he's out of the shop, then I might be able to find some kind of clue.

Now, my heart is thumping like the bass drum again. It echoes in my ears. At the same time, there's another sound in my head – a voice that's telling me I can do this. No one knows more about Amasi than I do. Pappy says that I'd make a good detective. I can solve this. The green police box draws me in like a magnet. It's where that protester was being kept; it's where the police ran to check. I feel like it has a connection, even though that guy was handcuffed and locked inside the whole time.

When I reach it, my luck is definitely in. I can see that the door to the box is not properly closed. A crack of light separates the door from the frame. All the police have gone. Everyone else around is walking by, minding their own business. Whoever was responsible didn't even shut it properly, let alone lock it back up behind them. If there's a clue to be found, this is my chance.

I glance up and down the road. Dada will be out of the shop soon and the moment will have passed. I edge my fingertips into the open crack, pull open the door and slip quickly inside, pulling the door shut again behind me.

Chapter Nine

The police box actually looks really cool inside. It's not big. I reckon if I lay down on the floor with my toes touching one end, I could reach my arms over my head and touch the wall at the other end. It's like being in a secret den while the noise of the world passes by outside. There's an old-fashioned phone attached to the wall with a cord that connects the receiver to the bit where you dial. There's a shelf with books: a couple of maps, a telephone directory, a city guide.

I sit down on a rickety, three-legged, wooden stool that's been stashed in the corner. It's covered in nicks and scratches but has a smooth seat, probably from many years of being sat on. I'm trying to imagine what that protester would have been thinking and seeing in here.

I can feel my breath finally returning to normal after my sprint across the road. I do feel a little bit guilty. I know I shouldn't have run off without telling Dada but I don't think he'd have agreed to be the Doctor Watson to my effort at Sherlock Holmes. If I can think quickly, I'll be back outside the newsagents before he's served.

My eyes dart around. Two sides of this box are right up against the corner brick walls of the town hall. There are a couple of windows but they have dusty pieces of cardboard taped to all of the panes. The tape is yellow and dry but the card covers all the glass and doesn't let in much light. There's a window in the door, too, but it has a kind of frosted glass, like our bathroom window. My feet dangle down while sitting on the stool and I look at them swinging underneath me. The floor looks like concrete: hard, solid and grey. Above me, the roof curves in an arch but has no gaps or joins.

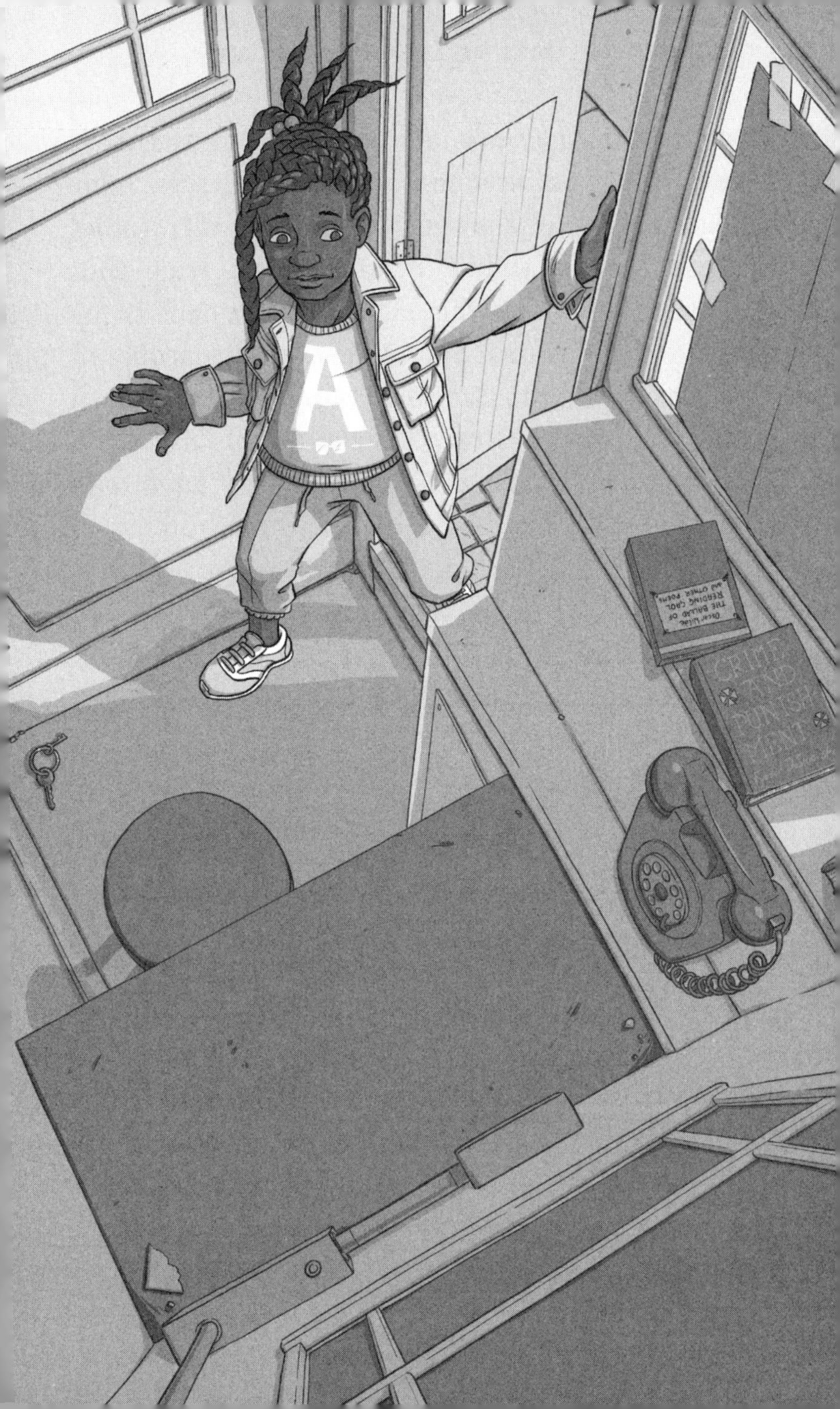
THE BALLAD OF
READING GAOL
and OTHER POEMS

It doesn't take me long to realise that there's definitely no escape route from inside here. No opening in the roof. No secret underground passageway. Unlike in the magic trick that Dada showed me this morning, this door is the only way in and out. A few small cardboard boxes are on the floor and I use my foot to push them along. They're full of other books and stuff, nothing interesting. I know I don't have long and I shouldn't be in here so I'm thinking of how to sneak back out. I can hear the constant footsteps of people who happen to be passing on the other side of the door. I can't risk Dada seeing me coming out of here.

Then, something shiny catches my eye near to where I've moved the box. When I bend down to pick it up, I see that it's a keyring with two keys: one bigger, copper-coloured key and one smaller, silver key. I turn them over in my hands. They're not dusty like the boxes and other things in here.

My first thought is the door but, as my eyes dart to near the handle, it's clear that there is nowhere for a key to be inserted on this side of the door. I put my ear to the panel to listen, in case anyone is immediately outside. There are people passing by but no voices. Carefully, I push open the door and peek through the tiniest gap. No sign of Dada. He must still be in the shop.

The coast seems to be as clear as it's likely to get. Keys still balled in my fist, I'm about to slither out of the narrowest opening I can manage. At exactly the wrong time, the door is caught by the breeze and the handle slips from my grasp. It swings open wildly as far as it will go on its hinges, blocking the view back up the road like a huge shield.

As quickly as I can, I grab it to pull it back. Behind it stands an old man wearing a flat cap, eyes wide open like a cartoon and steadying himself with his walking stick. The door must have just flown open in his face. Lucky he wasn't any closer or it might have knocked him clean off his shaky feet.

"Sorry," I mouth. I gently ease the door back into place behind me, leaning my back against the panel until it clicks into place. The old man stares at me for a moment, recovering from the shock. Without saying a word, he blinks and scratches his head and then carries on by with a *tut-tut.*

I wait for a moment as a few more groups of people pass. The flow of pedestrians then has a little gap. Still no sign of Dada coming out of the shop. I spin around and try shoving the bigger key into the lock. What d'you know? It works! A perfect fit. Quickly, I turn it and find that I've locked the door. I turn it the other way and unlock it. How strange – a key to the door was inside the box. A key that only works from the outside. My mind races. It feels like a clue and I feel like a detective. I have found this key while none of those police officers earlier thought to look. I *can* help to solve this mystery – but only if I can find some more clues.

Chapter Ten

Dada seems to be taking a while in the newsagents if he's only getting a drink. I wonder if there's a queue. Stepping over towards the shop, I peer inside but I can't see any customers. That's weird. Unless... maybe he came out of the shop while I was in the police box.

Uh-oh.

I pull my phone from my pocket as I begin to wander along Surrey Street, the way we were heading. Immediately, I see that there's a missed call on it from him. It must have been on silent. He's going to wonder where I am. I tap the notification to call him straight back but, when I put the phone to my ear, I just hear a busy tone. I wonder how I'm going to explain this.

"Demi!" I'm jolted from my thoughts as I hear my name shouted behind me. My first thought is Dada, but this is a girl's voice. I look towards where the voice came from and see a group of older girls. I recognise one of them from the tram. Among them, someone is looking straight at me.

"Celeste," I say as my shoulders sag. Her face is in some kind of permanent scowl. Maybe the wind changed direction once and she got stuck like that. She's the last person I want to see right now. "What are you doing here?"

"Demi! I thought it was you! Who are you with? I'm with my sister and her friends."

"I... I..." I look around and then can't seem to stop the lie from leaving my lips. I think of her teasing me just last week about not being allowed anywhere without an adult. "I'm here on my own. Came on the tram."

Celeste narrows her eyes, pinching her scowling features even more. She seems unconvinced but she can't argue with the fact that no one else is with me right now. It's the same look she gave me when I wore my pink sunglasses walking to school one morning. She told me they were babyish.

One of the friends then looks over Celeste's shoulder at me. "Hey. Were you here to see Amasi too?" she asks me with a kind smile.

I nod with a little confusion. Is this girl suggesting that they have come to see Amasi? Even Celeste, who has always said that I'm immature for liking her?

"Is that why you were all here as well?" I ask. She seems much nicer than Celeste.

"Yeah," says the girl.

"No," says Celeste. The other girl gives her an odd look. "No. I mean, not just that. Yeah, we were going along but just hanging out here, too. These are my sister's friends from college. I'm helping them with their media studies project. They're doing some street photography and stuff."

"But you don't like Amasi?" I say to Celeste and make it sound like a question so it's less of an accusation. I think of the times she's teased me and said that only little kids were into Amasi.

"Course she does," the girl replies on her behalf. Celeste looks sheepish and doesn't argue with the older girl. "We all love a bit of 'Follow Your Dreams', don't we, Cel?"

There's a pause but Celeste doesn't respond. She's got that scowl again but she's directing it at me so that her sister's friend can't see it.

"Hey, do you want to follow our page where we've been uploading our pics and stuff? We've got some cool shots from this morning. You might be on them somewhere! I'll give you the link if you like," the girl offers.

"Yeah," I reply. "Thanks, that would be awesome."

"It's mad what's happened with the guitar, though, hey?" she says as she shows me her phone with thumbnails of her photos and videos. We talk about how the story has unfolded. I tell them about the protester and the green police box. I talk mainly to the older girl, who seems really interested. Celeste doesn't say much. As I mention about me getting inside and finding the key, Celeste's sister butts into the conversation, too. I realise that the entire group of six girls are now listening. I feel like I'm giving a speech.

"Nice job! Right little detective, aren't you?" the sister declares with a grin, loudly chomping on some chewing gum.

"I just want to figure out what's happened," I respond. Even Celeste's sister is nicer than Celeste.

"You supposed to be going to the concert tonight?" she chomps.

"Yeah, of course," I say.

"Well, you'd better up the detective work, then. I just saw online that they're gonna cancel it if the guitar isn't found."

I think my mouth drops open. The older girls all look at me seriously.

"So, what are you gonna do next?" the sister asks, like she feels that it matters.

"Well, I figured it was worth going to find the tour bus round the back of the town hall."

"They're not gonna tell you anything, though, are they?" Celeste says.

"That's probably a good idea, actually," the first friend chips in, ignoring Celeste's comment. "Kassie's boyfriend says that the bus got diverted from the way it was supposed to come in. But then his friend saw them move the cones from the road as soon as the bus had been turned round, like they didn't really need to be there. There didn't seem to be any good reason for the road to be blocked off. Seems dodgy, if you ask me."

"And it was a real pain," another girl says. "We'd been waiting up near the barriers at the top of the Peace Gardens where it was supposed to arrive. We'd got there early and everything. Then, we totally missed it because it got sent the other way around to the back of the town hall."

There's a voice in my head now, saying: *Think like Sherlock. What would a real detective do? He would follow the evidence and look for clues*, I tell myself. The tour bus got diverted from where it was supposed to arrive. I wonder why. It should have been a big arrival where Celeste and her sister's friends were waiting. Instead, it had to approach round the back streets where it was much quieter. The last known place that the guitar was seen must have been on or near the bus, though. That's where to go.

Another thought comes to my mind: my phone. I was taking photos all morning on my phone, too. Maybe there's something there to help. I whip it back out of my pocket and now see *three* missed calls from Dada and another one from Pappy.

Oh, no! I got distracted and never switched the ringtone back on and it has still been on silent. Now I'm really going to need a good explanation.

A new message makes the phone vibrate in my hand.

Demi – Where r u? I'm by the bus! Call me!

Chapter Eleven

"Thanks. I've gotta go," I tell Celeste and the other girls.

"Good luck!" one of them says.

"Hope you find some more clues, detective," says another. Celeste just gives me her scowl.

I walk quickly back towards the road where the tour bus is parked. At least Dada has headed there, too. Once I get closer, I can call him back and tell him that I was looking for him there.

I can't wait to check my photos, though, and

begin to flick through as I walk. There are photos of the stage, the flag sellers, the crowd – not what I was hoping for, but then I was hardly going to come across a photo of someone caught red-handed nabbing Amasi's guitar. I go back again through the photos and videos I've been snapping all morning. There's the busker, the walking disco lady, the protesters...

Wait! Hold on a minute!

I flick back and forth between the picture of the busker who I gave some money to and the protester who the police put in the green box. Neither of my pictures show their faces properly but there's something odd. Their shoes are exactly the same – a brown, fabric look with a couple of white stripes. Not really uncommon I suppose but the jeans that they're wearing are identical, too: the same dark blue colour, the same rip across them, just above the left knee. It's like they are the same person: the busker in his black jacket and the noisy protester with the huge bag of placards who had pulled his green, furry hood up over his head as he was marched away.

That makes no sense, though. How could they be the same person? Maybe it's just a coincidence that their shoes and jeans are the same.

I flick again to a video I recorded of when those police officers were leading the protester away from the crowd. The protester and the officer holding on to him both seem to speak but the noise from the crowd makes it hard to hear anything that they say. I turn up the volume and listen again but the sound escapes into the city centre air. I play it once more and put the phone to my ear and then I hear it.

"All right, flower. Take it easy," the protester says to the police officer, squirming uncomfortably.

I'm hardly looking where I'm going as I walk and look down at my phone.

"Demi!" A stern voice is saying my name. It's Pappy's voice and he's right in front of me.

"Oh... uh..."

"Where on earth have you been? Dada called me to say he was looking for you and you weren't answering your phone. What were you thinking, Demetria? I've dashed round here thinking something bad has happened to you."

"I... um... I'm sorry. It was just..."

"Stay right there while I phone him back and say I've found you."

He puts his hand on my shoulder. He is in his police uniform and I feel like I'm in even more trouble than when he normally tells me off.

"Ayo, I've found her."

When he's told Dada where we are and finished the quick call, he bends down with one knee on the ground. He doesn't shout but I can tell that he's cross from the scowl spreading right across his face.

"What were you thinking, Dems? You had us really worried."

"I just wanted to help find what happened to the guitar. I was only gone a minute... then I got distracted... but I've found some clues!"

"Demi, you can't get involved with that. We are investigating it. You need to leave that to us."

"But... I *know* her. And you always say that I'd make a good detective. I can help!"

"This is serious, Dems. You might think that you know her because you see her through the Internet but that doesn't mean that you really know her. We're not just playing detective here. This is for real – not just a game."

I step back, hurt by his words. "Is that what you think I'm doing? Just playing a game?"

"No, that's not what I meant. It's just –"

Dada arrives out of breath and cuts him off. "Demetria," he says with equal full-name seriousness as Pappy. "Where did you get to? I came out of the shop and you were gone! You didn't answer your phone, then it was a busy tone and then no answer again."

"I'm sorry. It was on silent and I did try to call you back but then I bumped into some people and I've found some stuff out and –"

"Demi. What did I just say?" Pappy interrupts. "You need to leave it!"

I cross my arms in the most dramatic fashion that I can muster and accompany the movement with a huge sigh. They both just stare back at me.

Pappy still has his policeman's stern face on. Dada has this slightly more inquisitive look and I can tell that he's intrigued.

I focus my gaze on him, without saying anything. I raise my eyebrows in silent communication.

"Let's just hear her explanation," Dada suggests to Pappy, throwing me a lifeline. "Then, we'll draw a line under it."

Pappy crosses his arms. He doesn't reply but seems to give me the chance to speak.

"I think I know who took the guitar," I say clearly. "I think it was that protester."

"How, Dems? We saw him get locked in that police box," replies Dada. "Then, we saw it get opened and he was still in there – in handcuffs! It can't have been him. You said it yourself – you thought he'd escaped but he obviously hadn't."

"But... I found a key in there!"

"It doesn't matter. I know that box. You can't unlock it from the inside," says Pappy.

"Wait – you found a key? In the box? Are you saying you were inside?" Dada is the one to spot the obvious,

even though Pappy is the police officer.

"Yes, I was inside. And I know you can't unlock it from the inside. I checked. But it was the key to lock it from the outside and there was another smaller key with it. There's something not right. I just know it."

"Right, we've heard you out but you're going to have to let this drop, Dems," Pappy insists. "And I need to get back to work. I'm due back at the station now. I'm sure that man will be questioned but then he's likely to be ruled out of any further enquiries. Just forget about it."

Pappy gives Dada's hand a quick squeeze and smiles at him as he turns to leave. "Be careful," Dada says to him as always and Pappy leaves. It's just the two of us again.

"You've got to believe me, Dada. Please, can we just go to see the tour bus? Then, if there are no clues, I'll forget about it. I promise."

"You heard what Pappy said," he replies.

"Yeah. He said I was just playing detective. Is

that what you both think?"

"You know he doesn't mean it like that," says Dada.

"Then, let's just go and see the tour bus. That's where we were going anyway."

He gives me a look which tells me that I might have won him over.

"Your Pappy is going to go crazy if he finds out," Dada declares. Then, he flicks his head in the direction towards the back of the town hall. "What else have you discovered, then?"

Chapter Twelve

I scroll through the photos and videos on my phone again to show Dada as we walk. First, I show him the matching jeans and shoes of both the busker and protester. Then, I play the video of the protester being led away.

"Listen," I say and put the phone close to Dada's ear. "Does this sound familiar?"

Dada listens but looks at me and shrugs.

"That protester calls the police officer 'flower' when she's leading him away. That's exactly what the busker called me when I threw him some money. Plus, they have the same jeans and trainers and look the same height and everything," I babble. "I think they are the same person. But why would the busker suddenly be protesting and why did he swap his black coat for a green jacket?"

Dada gives me a long, quizzical look and I can't tell whether he's convinced or not. "Even if you're right and it's one person, that person was still locked up when the guitar went missing. Anyway, the tour bus is just round this corner. Better see what clues you can pull from here then, my little Sherlock!" He smiles.

Nick, the wiry man with the ponytail, is standing next to the bus. He's talking to three other guys who look in competition to see who can dress the scruffiest. There's a barrier separating us, with one of the event stewards standing proudly next to it in his hi-vis vest. I can't quite hear what they're saying.

"We need to get closer," I say.

"The barrier's here for a reason, Demi," Dada points out.

I look up at him with my cutest expression. He knows exactly what I'm trying to do.

"Pappy would definitely go crazy if he knew. How do I let you convince me of these things?" He shakes his head but the corner of his mouth is upturned. "Right – magician's distraction technique. On my signal, you sneak round the back. Be quick!"

He reaches inside his top pocket and then taps the steward on the arm. "Hey, mate. Pick a card, any card!"

I see my chance and nip under the barrier and round the other side of the bus. I edge along the side and then round the front, crouching down to stay hidden. The group are still chatting between themselves and now I can hear.

"So, lemme get this straight," Nick says to another guy who has equally long hair but no ponytail. The guy is scratching under his armpit and then sniffs his finger. "You definitely didn't unload the guitar from the bus?"

"No. I thought you'd unloaded it," armpit guy

replies. He wrinkles his nose at the smell of his own fingers and then shoves both hands into his frayed pockets. "You said up there on stage that you'd unloaded it."

"Did I?" Nick asks, with an expression that suggests he actually can't remember what he said. "I mean, I definitely took the case up on stage like I normally do. I don't think I took it off the bus, though." He rubs his hand down his bristly beard as he talks it through. "I'm sure it was already off. One of you must have unloaded it. I think I picked up the case from down here and just took it up next to the microphone stand like usual."

"Look, I definitely saw the guitar in the case when we were on the bus after you'd cleaned it," says a different guy with headphones over his ears. "Next I remember is you'd taken it up on stage."

"Hang on," chips in another one of the group, speaking with his mouth full of food. I didn't think he was even listening until now. He'd been munching through a bag of crisps but only half of them seemed to be making it into his mouth

– the other half were dropping down his T-shirt and hitting the floor. "If none of us unloaded the guitar or the case, how did the empty case even get down here before being carried on stage?"

They all look at each other with blank expressions.

I spot the opportunity to sneak back out to Dada. The steward is shrugging his shoulders and laughing. Dada taps one finger on the side of his nose and pockets his deck of cards again.

"That's magic," he says with a grin.

"But how did you..." the steward's voice tails off.

"What've you found out?" Dada asks me as we turn and leave the man open-mouthed and scratching his head.

"None of them can remember unloading the guitar from the bus. They don't have a clue!" I exclaim.

"Come on," he says. "Let's walk and you can

fill me in."

We wander up towards the fountain outside City Hall where we like to sit and eat cake from the nearby cafe. I tell him about the conversation and the confusion between the crew. "It makes no sense," I say between bites of my favourite – a chocolate eclair. "Somehow, it was there in the case on the bus but when the case was taken onto the stage, the guitar had gone."

"Maybe it's best to let the professionals do their job, hey, Dems?"

"What if they can't solve it? What if the guitar isn't found and the concert is cancelled and all because we missed something that could have helped?"

"I know you mean well, but you've done your best. There's only so far you can get from knowing all of Amasi's songs and videos and her insta-whatsit posts –"

"That's it!"

"That's what?"

Dada's rambling reminded me of Amasi's website, where she's always vlogging and posting videos behind the scenes. I haven't checked on there today. Maybe there will be something. I'm racing to catch up with my own thoughts as I swipe through my phone to the browser app. Yes – there are two new videos posted today!

The first has a close-up selfie shot of Amasi as the thumbnail and the caption 'Yass! Excited, much!' The timestamp says it was from early this morning, though. The second grabs my attention. The tour bus is in the thumbnail with the caption 'Finally arrived! Let's do this!'

I hit play and the video fills my phone screen. Dada leans over my shoulder and cranes his neck to watch, too. Amasi's voice is narrating as the camera focus shakily bobs around. It's following the smartly dressed woman who was on stage earlier. I think she might be the tour manager or agent. First, the video is from behind her as she steps down from the bus. Then, she turns around and the camera zooms in for an extreme close-up before she pushes it away playfully. The shot swings round and I can see Ponytail Nick and another guy lifting a metal crate from the luggage hold underneath the bus. The other guys that I saw at the tour bus are milling around carrying boxes and wires and bags. Everyone seems in a rush.

Then, I see it – just a glimpse at the edge of the frame.

It's someone carrying Amasi's purple guitar case. They're in shot for only a second so it's impossible to know where they're carrying it to or from. They're just passing the side of the bus, as are a bunch of the crew. I can see one thing for sure, though. It might have been a quick glimpse but there were those same brown shoes and dark blue, ripped jeans.

"Did you see that?" I ask Dada.

"Show me again," he says.

As we watch for a second time, I double-tap the screen to zoom in. The picture gets a bit bigger but more blurry.

"That's definitely the same jeans and shoes that

the protester was wearing – and the busker. Is this one of them? Are they all the same person?" I'm saying it partly to Dada and partly just thinking out loud. My heart is thumping away at the thought of another useful discovery. At the same time, my brain is whizzing in circles trying to figure out what it means.

"Well, whoever it is, it looks like they definitely have the guitar case," Dada replies.

"Hang on!" I play and pause the video again and again, stopping to catch the frame at the precise moment.

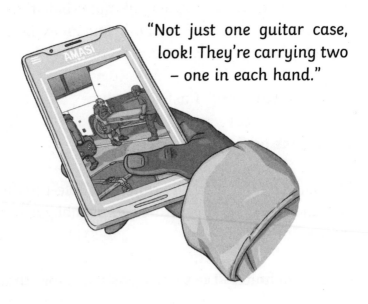

"Not just one guitar case, look! They're carrying two – one in each hand."

Chapter Thirteen

"This is proof!" I stand up and look at Dada, who is still sitting on the edge of the fountain.

"Well, slow down a minute," he says. "Proof of what, exactly? What does it prove? It's just someone carrying the guitar case. It doesn't mean they took the guitar. It doesn't show they've done anything wrong."

"It's a clue, though. Don't you see? This is the protester. He has the same green jacket, the jeans, everything."

"You're forgetting one thing, Dems. Look at the

timestamp on the video. That's exactly when that protester was locked in the police box. If anything, this proves that it's *not* him. That person carrying the guitar cases cannot possibly be the same person who was locked inside the police box. No one can be in two places at once."

I stare at the paused video and tap my fingers on the edge of my phone. Dada is right. My brain is still whizzing.

What would Sherlock do? I think again. A good detective makes connections, uses everything they know and joins the dots.

"I've seen that other guitar case before," I blurt out as the realisation dawns on me.

"Really? Where?"

I swipe to switch phone apps and go back to my photos, flicking through until I reach a picture of the busker. His guitar case is laid out in front of him, collecting coins like the ones I'd thrown in for him. On the side of it are a bunch of tatty stickers.

"There it is!" I say proudly. "Same stickers. I'm telling you – that busker and that protester are the same person. And whoever they are, they're in Amasi's video with her guitar case and the guitar case I threw a coin into this morning."

"This still doesn't make sense to me, though, Dems. Let's think about it for a minute. We saw the protester handcuffed and locked into the police box. The guitar was stolen by someone two streets away, round the corner. Then, after this had happened, we saw the same protester, still handcuffed, still in the box. How can that be?"

I had to admit, I couldn't answer that. It felt like climbing the ladder on a board game only to slither back down a snake. Or like a jigsaw with important pieces missing.

"OK, what else do we know?" Dada was starting to sound as much of a detective as me. Maybe Pappy would be proud of us both after all.

"Right, let's think. The protester was shouting about stopping the concert, bad-mouthing Amasi. He was arrested and locked in the green police box..."

"But you said you found a key in there?"

"Yes, I did! Two keys but the one for the door couldn't be used from the inside so it wasn't any use to escape with." I felt like I was on a roll again. I was in full detective mode, analysing the case. Maybe Dada could be my Doctor Watson after all.

"OK, go on – what else?"

"From the photos I took on my phone, it looks like the protester was also busking this morning, playing a guitar. We gave him some money. He must have changed his jacket but his jeans and shoes are identical. The same guy is in Amasi's vlog carrying his own guitar case and hers." My hands are waving around as I go back over the details. I'm hoping that saying them out loud might just lead to a discovery. It works for real detectives when they're explaining a case so it's worth a try.

"But the crew said they didn't know who unloaded the guitar," Dada reminds me.

"Exactly. So maybe he somehow sneaked among them, blending in. He already had one guitar case of his own. He's taken Amasi's from the storage of the bus and just not been noticed."

"Perhaps it's a case of the old switcheroo! What if this guitar case" – Dada points at the black case with the stickers on – "was empty and this one" – he points at the gleaming, purple case in the man's other hand – "still had Amasi's guitar in? At some point between it coming off the bus and being carried on stage, he just needed to get Amasi's guitar out of that purple case and into the empty, black one."

"Always thinking like a magician, aren't you, Dada? I think you might be right. But that would mean his own guitar that he was playing earlier must have been left somewhere," I ponder out loud again.

"All this is possible but it still doesn't work because the protester couldn't be in two places at once. We know he was still in the box when the police came to check. We saw it!"

"We know he was in there afterwards," I say. "And we know he could get back in if he had that key to unlock it from the outside."

"But he couldn't get out if the key didn't work from the inside."

"So, maybe we still need to think like a magician again," I offer. "What if he was not even in the box when it got locked?"

"Huh?" Dada clearly wasn't following me, yet.

"It's the classic magician trick, isn't it? Just like what you were showing me earlier. Fool the audience into thinking something. When that magician showed his assistant getting into the wardrobe, we saw afterwards she was just stepping right through and out the back."

"Yeah but that contraption had a false back panel and a secret door. There was no other way out of this police box."

"So, instead of stepping right through, he sneaked away while covered by the door. He could easily have hidden behind a phone box or a parked car until the coast was completely clear. Everyone is thinking he was in the box and can't figure out how he escaped. Maybe he never got in the box in the first place. Maybe the big key was to let himself in later, after he stole the guitar."

"That's smart thinking, Dems. And I guess we're both thinking the same thing about what the little key was for."

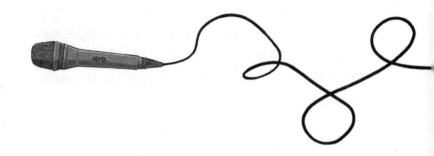

Chapter Fourteen

"The handcuffs," I nod as I reply to Dada. Little thoughts keep exploding like popping candy in my head. "If the little key fitted the handcuffs, he could unlock them and just put them back on again afterwards to pretend they'd been on all the time."

The whole possibility seems to be gradually absorbed by Dada. Wrinkles spread across his forehead and his eyebrows wriggle like caterpillars. Just when I think I've convinced him, he shakes his head. "Nah! It can't be that," he says.

"What d'you mean? Why not?"

"Well, for a start, that would mean the police officer who put him in there must have been in on the whole thing. She'd have had to provide him with the keys. I thought you saw her bundle him inside with a struggle? You watched on my shoulders, remember?"

It's true. I did watch from his shoulders. I go back over it in my mind. The police officer opened the door wide. I could see her scrabbling to get him inside. I could see her but I couldn't see him. He was blocked by the open door. After seeming to struggle, she pushed the door closed and leant herself against it. Of course, I assumed he was inside then. But what if it was all a distraction to let him slip away, with the cover of the wide-open door blocking the view for me and the rest of the crowd?

I think back to the startled, old man who I hit when I came out of the box. I didn't even see him when the door swung open and he didn't see me. The door was like a huge shield blocking the view.

I swipe through my phone photos again, hoping to spot something I haven't already noticed. Nothing new jumps out. I've looked at all my pictures over and over, now. Then, I remember – I haven't been the only one taking photos this morning. Celeste's sister and friends have been uploading their photos. That girl showed them to me and told me the link to view them. What was it for? Their media studies project at college, I think she said.

My fingers work speedily to tap in the address into my search bar.

Bingo!

A whole page of thumbnails. I instantly recognise tiny versions of the scenes from the Peace Gardens, Fargate and the town hall. My eyes scan through them all, squinting to pick out details before choosing any to click and enlarge.

Nothing looks likely to be any more help than my own photos that I've already checked, until... a row of three tiny pictures of that spot where the busker was playing his sad version of

'Follow Your Dreams'.

I tap to bring up the enlarged version of the first photo. "Look. That's the busker talking to the police officer. What was she called? PC Mullins?" She's crouched down and the two of them are talking really close together like they know each other...

"So, if the busker is also the protester, then he had spoken to that officer before," Dada confirms. "They knew each other before she even arrested him. That does seem shifty but that doesn't make it a crime."

I swipe to the next photo. "Now, see? Same spot but after we'd passed the busker. According to the time in the filename, this picture is from half an hour later and he's gone but his guitar case and jacket are propped against the wall."

"I guess that's when he was causing a fuss with the protest," Dada suggests.

I swipe again to the third photo in the set. I squint my eyes again as I take in what appears. It's the first time I've been able to see a clear shot of the busker's face. I pinch my finger and thumb on the image and zoom in. A lump catches in my throat but then so much becomes clear in my mind.

"I know who that is!" I say.

"What? Really?"

"Yes! We have to tell Pappy! I'll explain on the way."

Chapter Fifteen

"OK. Slow down a tad. He's not going to be pleased that I've been letting you investigate!"

"Not just letting me!" I tell Dada. "You've been investigating, too. We might have solved it between us. Can you call Pappy? He said he was due back at the station. Tell him we're on our way."

Dada gives me this look which says that he kind of disapproves but that he's giving in anyway. He tries Pappy's phone but there's no answer. We set off towards the tram stop. "Can't we get a taxi?" I suggest. Dada insists that the tram will be just as quick with the city centre traffic to contend with on the roads. That means waiting, though. I dance from foot to foot as I tell Dada who the busker is. I should have realised it sooner. We walk back down Fargate and I pause.

"If I'm right about this, it could mean that he stashed his own guitar somewhere so that he had an empty case. In fact, after he made the swap, he might have even ditched his guitar case, too, because it would be easier to hide the stolen guitar loose in that huge bag of his..."

As I'm saying it, I pull Dada's arm, taking him in the direction of the side road of Surrey Street again.

"We've been down here, Dems. I thought you were in a hurry to get to Pappy!"

"I am! Let's just check, though. If he's stashed his old guitar, it would have to be down here between the green police box and the corner of Norfolk Street where the tour bus was."

"There's nowhere down here that could –"

"In there!" I shout as it comes to me. I point towards two of those huge, metal bins with green, plastic lids. They sit together, side by side.

I heave open the first lid and push it back against the wall. Inside, it's piled with stinking rubbish. It makes me feel sick and I don't want to touch any of it but I have to check if I'm right. I push aside an open burger box with half of its unfinished contents spilling out. There are empty bottles and plastic bags filled with rubbish but no sign of anything else. My heart sinks a bit as I think that maybe this was a crazy suggestion.

I open the lid of the second with help from Dada. At least this one is not so messy as it's piled with cardboard. I push around the loose sheets on top... and there it is. Lying on a bed of flattened cardboard is the black guitar case with the tatty stickers, belonging to the busker.

Dada looks at it and looks at me and says, "I don't believe it! You were right!"

"Should we leave it here or take it out?" I ask.

"Don't touch it. It could be used as evidence, maybe. Looks like he's just stashed his old guitar case here. Your theory is spot on – easier to keep the stolen guitar loose in his bag. Just leave that cardboard on top and let's get to the station as quickly as we can."

We walk so fast that we're virtually running to the tram stop outside the cathedral and see the tram pulling in as we get there. We jump on board. It snakes its way far too slowly through the city centre and out towards the factories and warehouses on the east side of the city. When the doors open for us to get out, I run ahead but Dada shouts to slow down and wait for him.

I know the station where Pappy works because he's shown me before. Those were times when we'd just gone by together, though, not when he's actually been working. We are never supposed to bother him at work – and we've already called him away once today.

At the desk, Dada and I breathlessly charge in. The forehead of the bald man behind the desk creases as he sees us enter.

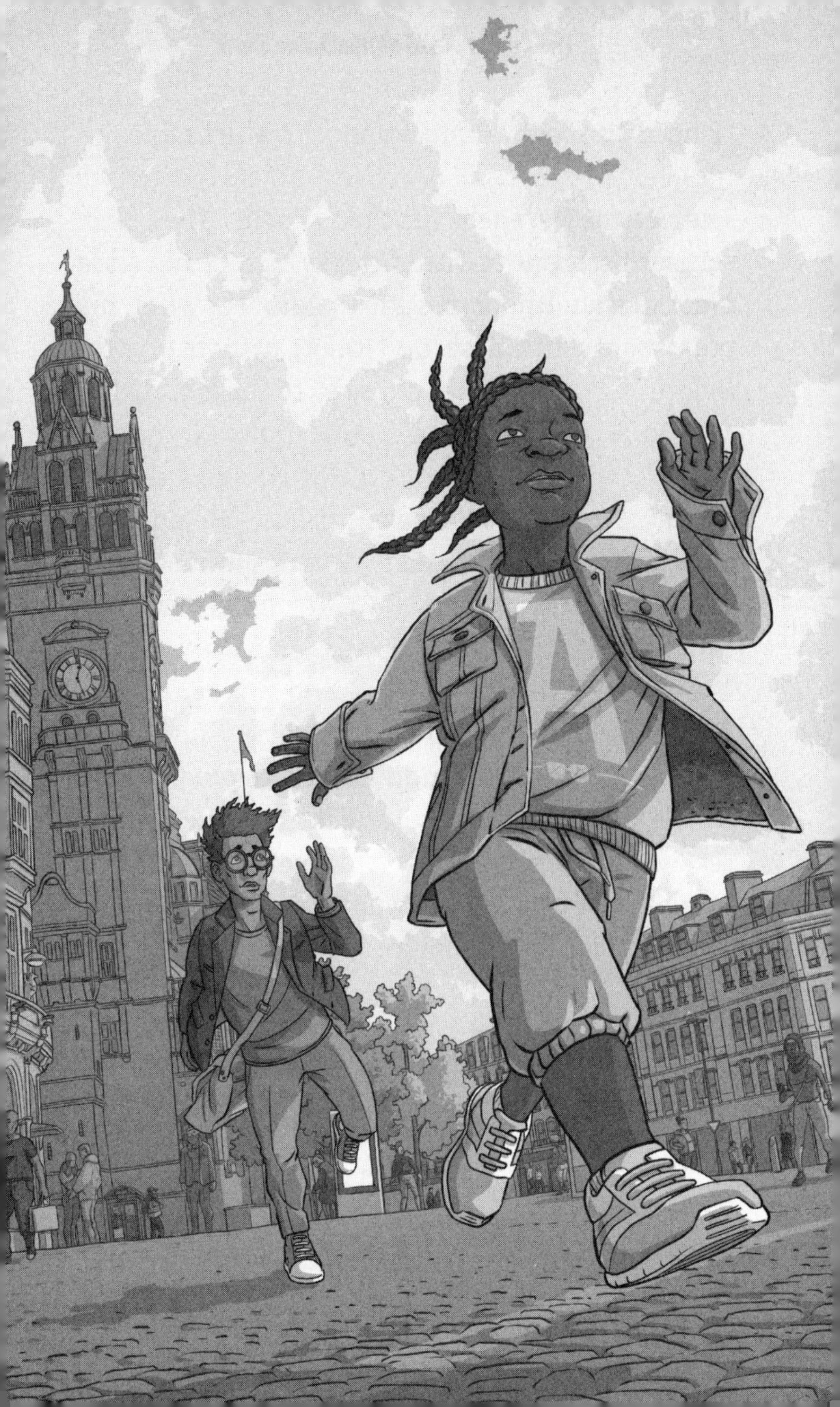

"I need to speak to my Pappy!" I blurt out.

The creases reach farther down the desk sergeant's brow towards the bridge of his nose and stretch up across his head. He puts his palms onto the desk and takes a long breath. Before he takes the chance to speak, Dada cuts in.

"Ahem, I'm sorry. Please excuse us." He puts his arm around my shoulder. "What she means is, do you happen to know if PC Akpan is available by any chance?"

"Dada, tell him it's an emergency!" I shoot a glance up at him. Dada smiles apologetically to the desk sergeant who picks up a telephone receiver in front of him. He doesn't take his eyes off us as he prods some numbers into the phone and then waits a moment.

"PC Akpan," he says into the phone. "Someone at the front desk for you. Young girl says it's an emergency. I believe it's your daughter." He places the phone back in its cradle and tells us to take a seat. We walk over to the plastic seating and Dada mutters at me to calm down.

Pappy's face appears through the glass window of a thick, blue door before he pushes it open and steps through to the waiting area. I can't tell if he's mad or worried at seeing us there. I jump out of my seat and start babbling too quickly.

"I've figured it out. I was checking my phone for pictures and... and... I've seen Amasi's vlog and these other pictures from Celeste's sister's friends. Plus, we listened to the backstage crew because I sneaked under the barrier and anyway they didn't know but I know who took the guitar and you won't believe it but –"

"Woah, woah, woah!" says Pappy, holding his hands like he's trying to stop traffic and not just my barrage of words. "What's this about? Have you come all the way over here to tell me about this Amasi guitar business?"

He looks at Dada and his face definitely gives more of a cross expression than worried. Dada shrugs his shoulders and is about to speak but I don't let him before I carry on, tugging on Pappy's arm.

"Please, Pappy, you have to listen. That protester is the same man who was busking earlier and we gave him money and he called me 'flower' and then he said the same to that police officer who arrested him and he was talking to her earlier but I know who he is now and I think she's helping him, so..."

Pappy cuts me off again, this time shushing me and stepping between me and the desk sergeant who is watching our conversation unfold with eyes like a hawk.

"Keep it down, Demi. Will you just slow down and think about what you're saying for a minute? This is really serious and I told you not to get involved. I really need to get back to work. I know you mean well but..."

Pappy turns away, shaking his head. He strides back towards the door he just came through.

My heart sinks.

Chapter Sixteen

"Wait," says Dada to Pappy. "You should hear what Demi has to say."

Pappy has swiped his identity card at the side of the door and pulled it open. He holds the handle with one hand as he looks back at Dada and then me. He chews the thought around for a moment. The desk sergeant raises an eyebrow.

"Fine. Come through here for a minute and get it off your chest – but make it quick." He leads us through the door and into a little room with a small sofa, a table and a couple of rough fabric chairs. I sit on the edge of the sofa, Dada takes a chair and Pappy stands with his arms folded.

I rattle through all of the clues and the evidence: the photos and videos of the busker and protester; overhearing the tour bus crew; the keys in the police box; the stashed guitar case in one of the bins; plus, of course, PC Mullins' involvement. It all comes tumbling out of my mouth with barely a breath in-between.

"So, if all that you're saying is true, you're suggesting that the stolen guitar is now in the bag with the placards the protester was carrying when he was brought to the station? That bag will have been checked at the scene and again when he was brought into custody."

"Yeah, *checked* by PC Mullins!" I say, making little air quotes around the word 'checked' to suggest that she didn't properly check at all or that she knew it was there and was purposely overlooking it.

"That's preposterous. It would mean that the currently most wanted item in the whole of Sheffield, that half the force is out there trying to locate, is –"

"... right here at the police station!" I finish the sentence.

"You don't mean to say that he could have just kept it with him here?" Dada asks.

"Not on his person, no," said Pappy. "The arresting officer – PC Mullins – would have checked the bag into a holding area while the suspect was being held for questioning."

"See?" I insist. "PC Mullins again. She's always there!"

Pappy puts his hands on his hips and shakes his head. "Obviously, under normal circumstances, that check would have revealed what was in the bag, but if you're right and PC Mullins is somehow involved, then she could have kept it from being seen by anyone else and just handled it herself. This is a really serious accusation, though." Pappy scratches his head as he processes all of the information.

"So, what would happen to the bag next?" Dada asks.

"Well, I suppose if – or when – the suspect was released, then he would get his belongings back from the holding area as he left."

"You can't let him leave now, Pappy. You have to check."

"I can't just go accusing another officer of something like this, either, Dems. I don't have anything other than your theory."

"But the theory is based on all the evidence," I plead. "I'm right. I *know* I am."

Still standing, Pappy rests his elbow in one hand and rubs his chin with the other. Just then, the door to the little room edges open. The head and hand of another police officer appears in the gap. I recognise her as the partner that Pappy usually works with.

"Everything OK in here?" the lady asks.

"Hmm, yeah," Pappy says with a lingering sigh. "Just one thing, Paula. Do you know what the status is of the guy brought in for causing a fuss at the Amasi launch event?"

"Oh, yeah," replies the officer cheerily. "Funny you should mention it. He's just being released. Hope he's not off to start another protest. He's just getting signed out."

Chapter Seventeen

"You're kidding!" Pappy exclaims.

"No, all done and dusted. Mullins questioned him. Just a caution for disturbing the peace. Nothing else to hold him on, apparently."

"Mullins," Pappy mutters. He looks at us. My eyes nearly pop out in despair. The other police officer stares at us in confusion.

"We've got to stop him!" I yell.

"I can't just rearrest him, Dems. Listen to what I just said."

"But he's probably got the guitar right now. We have to check!"

"Well, *we* don't have to, but PC Taylor and I could go and have a word." He turns to the officer still poking her head round the open door, eyebrows raised, wondering what the problem is. "Paula, have you got a minute to give me a hand? This is a bit delicate."

We all pile out of the room, through the corridor and out into the waiting area at the front. The protester is right there, standing at the desk that we approached when we arrived.

Strapped on his back, sure enough, is the huge bag that he had earlier. Two placard posts still poke up out of the top. I scrunch my eyes to scrutinise the shape of the bag. It bulges at the bottom with something curved, not just a flat, rectangular placard. That shape could definitely be a guitar.

He's not in handcuffs any more. Instead, he appears to be just signing a form on the desk with that same officer, PC Mullins, standing next to him. It can't just be a coincidence that she's always there.

Dada is standing behind me but puts his arms over my shoulders and locks his hands together in front of my chest. He must think I'm going to charge like a bull and he's got me strapped to him just in case. Pappy strides the few metres towards the desk with PC Taylor by his side.

"Excuse me, PC Mullins. I don't mean to interrupt. Is this your suspect?" Pappy asks.

"No longer a suspect. He's just leaving," PC Mullins responds, forcing a smile.

"So I gather. It's just," he clears his throat, "something just came to light and I wanted to double-check that the bag has been searched and the contents accounted for."

I am sure that I see a teeny change of expression in PC Mullins' face. Her eyes narrow. She definitely exchanges a quick look with the protester before answering. "Everything is accounted for, PC Akpan. I'm not sure what you think the problem is," she replies sharply.

"I'm sure there's no problem," Pappy states. "Perhaps PC Taylor and I could just confirm what's in the bag."

The protester – who I know is also the busker – takes a small step back. He seems to edge himself behind PC Mullins as if she will protect him. Still, she sticks to her guns and there's a kind of standoff between the two police officers – her and my dad.

Pappy turns to the desk sergeant with the bald head. The creases either never left the sergeant's head or they just return when I look at him.

"I'm sure you'd agree, Sergeant," says Pappy, "that if there's nothing to hide here, then the bag can be checked just before this man is released from custody."

The desk sergeant has the look of a man who doesn't really understand what is going on and doesn't really want to take a side. He sticks out his bottom lip and simply nods.

"I really don't think –" PC Mullins begins.

"You said there wouldn't be a problem, Sis," the protester interrupts.

Before she's quick enough to shush him, the implication of his words strikes us all one by one. I look up to Dada. Dada's mouth drops open. Pappy's face turns to a scowl.

"PC Mullins, did this man call you 'Sis'? Is this your brother? Because that would clearly represent a conflict of interest."

"Whatever you might think you know, PC Akpan, there's really nothing to see here," she replies, ignoring the question.

"I think we can all be the judge of that, then. Could we have the bag please, sir?" Pappy addresses the protester who looks again despairingly at PC Mullins.

Whatever silent understanding is being passed between them, the protester sighs and wriggles the straps of the bag off his shoulders and then sets it down carefully on the floor in front of him. I think of the similar-looking netball bag again at school, plonked in the middle of the playground with the mountain of balls inside making it stand upright. This bag leans to one side a little with the two placard posts now pointing out at an angle.

Pappy bends down and pulls the drawstring top to open it up. He looks straight back at me. The corner of his mouth twitches. As he wriggles the top of the bag down a little, the neck of a guitar also pokes out of the top.

"Well, would you believe it," he mutters quietly before addressing the whole room more loudly. "PC Taylor, get some handcuffs and detain this man. PC Mullins, I think you've probably got some explaining of your own to do. Sergeant, I think we should get the word out: we've found our stolen guitar."

With a flourish, he produces the guitar from the bag, lifting it carefully out...

...but it's not purple.

Even worse, it doesn't gleam and there's definitely no sign of any diamonds. It is the battered, old, brown guitar that the busker was playing this morning when I threw him some coins. I look at the man – the busker, the protester – who stares back at me with the same smug grin he had when the police found him still in that green box.

"Clearly, this is not the guitar that PC Akpan thought it was," says PC Mullins with a haughty expression. "I appreciate you witnessing this, Sergeant. I trust that it will be dealt with later. I'm going to get this man released and drop him back at his home address over the other side of Meadowhall."

She opens the door and the busking protester swipes up his bag with the guitar back inside. Before anyone dares to object, they're gone. I dip my head to my chest but peer up slowly to meet Pappy's gaze. I know he's looking at me because I can feel it burning into me.

"You need to go home, Demetria. We'll all talk later, Ayo. This has caused me a really serious problem."

Dada ushers me to the door without saying a word.

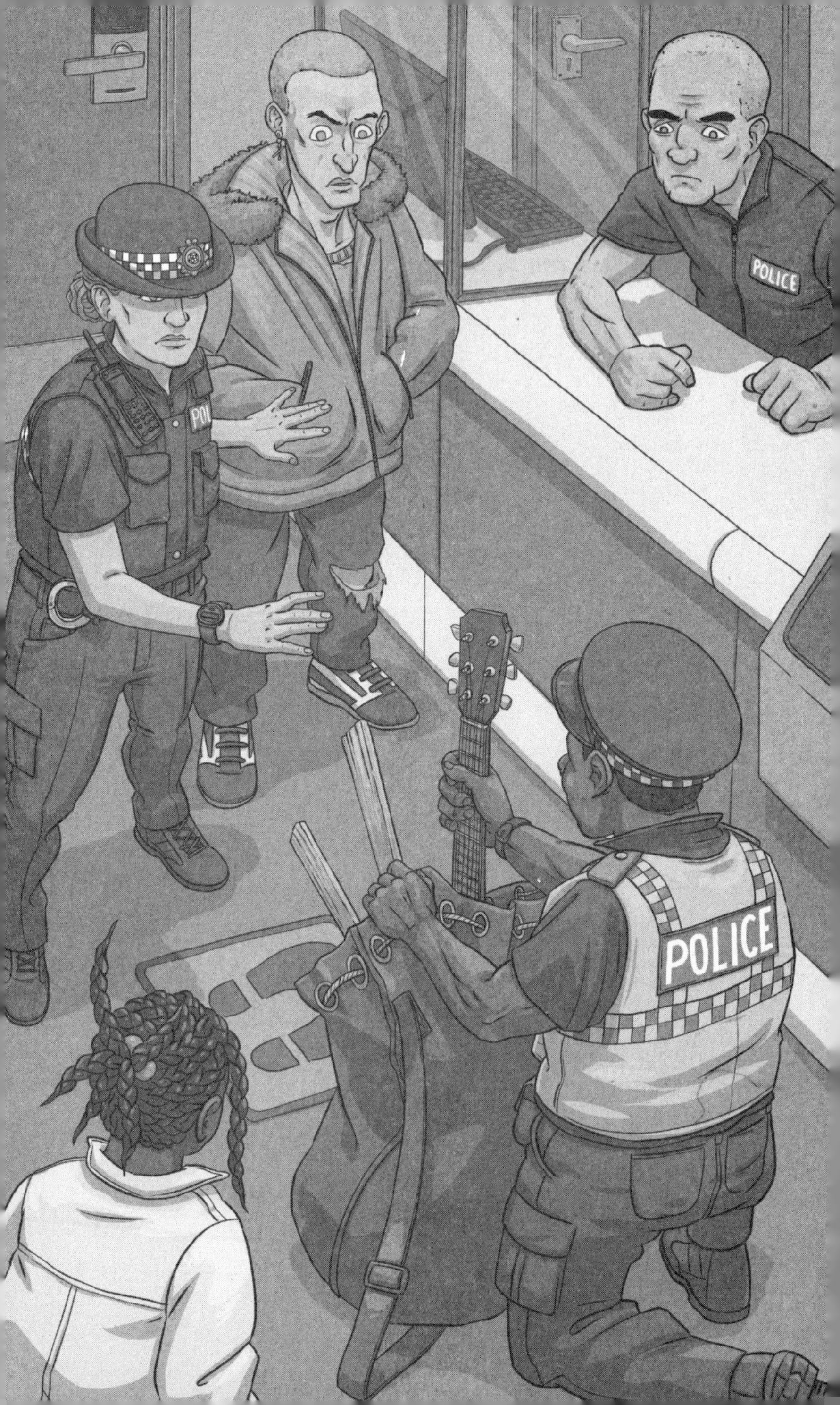
POLICE
POLICE

"But he called her 'Sis'. It doesn't add up. See that look on his face? He must..." I try one last plea as we're going out of the station but Pappy doesn't let me finish.

"Go home, Demi."

Chapter Eighteen

The station door closes behind us and we walk a little further from the entrance. I can feel tears welling up. I blink them away but all it does is release them down my cheeks. Dada gives me a hug and I sniffle all over his front.

"He must..." I sniffle again and try to get my words out but it's hard to catch my breath between sobs. PC Mullins has got into a police car with the protester in the passenger seat.

"Shh. It's all right, Dems. Calm down."

"He must have..." I shake my head as I'm

searching for the words. I feel like the thought of something just whooshed through me but I can't grasp it. The tears have blurred my thoughts as well as my eyes. I watch the police car pull out of the car park and turn left, heading towards Meadowhall shopping centre.

"Demi. Breathe." Dada lets go but crouches down to look at me. Over his shoulder, through the glass front of the police station, I see Pappy standing by the reception desk, his arms folded and his lips pursed. "We tried. You saw what was in the bag. It was his own guitar. We got it wrong."

"He must have stashed Amasi's guitar somewhere else. It must have been him," I sob, taking big gulps of air to catch my breathing up.

"Have a sip of my drink. You're so worked up," Dada says, passing me his bottle. I take a sip and try to calm down. Then, I notice that the police car has gone round the roundabout and is heading past the front of the station again in the opposite direction.

"Of course!" I blurt out as I point at the car

going by. "I know where it is! Why didn't we realise?" I glance back at the police station but Pappy is no longer standing by the reception desk. He's not seen the car turn around.

"What?" Dada is not on my wavelength again yet.

"Look! She said she was taking him home but Meadowhall is that way. They're heading back towards the city centre. We need to get back there," I plead as my thoughts begin to clear.

"I really don't think that's a good idea," Dada says but I quickly explain what I've realised.

"If that's where the guitar is, the protester is probably on his way right back there now to pick it up – and PC Mullins is gonna be helping him by taking him straight to it!" I finish.

"OK, here's the deal. Right now, Pappy is absolutely fuming. If we do this and we're right, we might just redeem ourselves. If we're wrong, we head straight back home and just forget about the guitar. Got it?"

"But if we forget about the guitar, what about

the concert?"

"If we're right, we're going to save the concert. If we're wrong, it'll be too late to worry about that. It's going to be in the hands of the experts. Now, you got that?"

"Let's do it," I say.

Without another word, we're both running back towards the tram stop. Minutes later, we're back on the tram for the third time today, heading back towards the city again. At the cathedral, we're running back along the pavement before Dada grabs my arm to stop me and check the traffic. As soon as we're safely across, we're sprinting now, back up Fargate, round the corner into Surrey Street, past the green police box and the newsagents.

I'm breathing so hard as I start to slow down that it feels like my lungs are going to explode. I look back over my shoulder and Dada is right behind me. We begin to walk and catch our breath together. Then, he stops me with his arm.

"Look!" he points to the green bins. A police car

is parked at the side of them and the protester has just got out of the passenger seat. He goes straight to the bin with the cardboard and opens the lid.

"Stop!" I shout and start running towards him again before Dada has a chance to pull me back. The noise I'm making catches his attention and he stops short of rummaging in the bin to look at me.

"You again!" he says furiously. I stop a few metres away from him. Now I see PC Mullins standing next to the police car.

"You're Berry. You used to be in the duo with Amasi, didn't you?" I ask the protester.

I already know the answer. When I finally caught a good look at his face in one of those pictures, I recognised him. The duo never had much success but I followed Amasi's rise to fame even in those early days.

The man tilts his head as he stares back at me. His fury softens slightly until a look of confusion spreads across his face. "What? How? You know me from then?" he asks, stuttering. "No one ever recognises me any more."

"Is that why you took the guitar?"

"I haven't got the guitar. We just proved that at the station. Now, get away from me or my sister will arrest you for harassing me."

"So, she *is* your sister. I know you took the guitar and it's in that bin, isn't it? Inside your old guitar case. Is it because you're jealous that Amasi has become so famous?"

"Hmph!" he snorts. "Famous. Successful. Popular. Rich. You name it. Me? I'm just stuck busking on the streets with most people walking by and not even noticing me."

"You admit it, then. That's not a reason to sabotage her, though," I say.

"I don't care. This is the least I deserve and you can't prove anything," he spits back at me and reaches back inside the bin.

"Don't be so sure about that," comes a familiar

voice from behind me.

"Pappy!" I spin around and cry out. "What are you doing here?"

"I had the same thought as you as soon as you left. I saw you point out the patrol car going back past the station in the opposite direction. I went back over everything you'd said and I knew you were right. The clincher was when we checked this morning's log and found that PC Mullins arranged a roadblock which diverted the tour bus to the more secluded location. No one else had any explanation about a roadblock – it must have been just part of their plan."

Dada puts his arm around me and gives me a squeeze as he looks across at the guilty police officer. PC Taylor catches up and goes straight over to PC Mullins at the side of the police car. Her shoulders sag and she puts her hands over her face. Pappy steps slowly closer to where the protester is standing and stares at him, waiting.

"Do you want to reach in and take out that case or shall I?" Pappy says to him. There's no answer, though, so the protester quickly finds handcuffs being placed on him for the second time today.

"OK, OK. It was wrong, I know. I shouldn't have done it." Berry crumbles as Pappy sits him on the ground. He leans back on the side of the bin as his head drops and his chin touches his chest. When Pappy has made sure that the handcuffs are secure, he carefully lifts the guitar case out of the bin and places it on the ground. With two flicks of the catches, he lifts it open.

The diamond-encrusted outer casing of Amasi's guitar reflects the sunlight so it appears as if flashing laser beams are being flung from it in every direction. Years' worth of music and memories are encased in this instrument. It's so precious and I know how much it means regardless of the sparkling gems.

"Wow!" is all I can manage.

"Please, I didn't do any harm. I just saw all the publicity she was getting for this homecoming and world tour and it didn't seem fair. I wanted it just as much as she did. Why did she get everything and I got nothing?" the man rambles.

"Well, you got something," Pappy chips in. "You've probably earned yourself a criminal conviction. As for you, PC Mullins... I can only imagine what an internal investigation will decide to do about your involvement. It's totally unacceptable for a serving officer. What were you thinking?"

"I know I'll probably lose my job over this but he's my brother. We never did anything to hurt anyone. He just wanted to be noticed and needed again. I would have made sure he returned the guitar. He was only disrupting the concert, not actually stealing it."

"Well, I'm not sure that everyone will see it that way, but that's not for us to decide right now. I think the next step is for us to get this beloved guitar back into the hands of the person that owns it. What do you say, Demi?"

I look at Pappy and decipher what he means. By 'us', does he mean me, too? Am I returning the guitar? I look at Dada, too, and he flashes me a huge smile.

Chapter Nineteen

It is still Saturday – but only just. It's not far from midnight.

Not only did we manage to solve the mystery of the missing guitar but we found it in time to save the concert. I was the detective that pieced all the clues together – with a little help from Dada, maybe! Without me, Pappy admitted, the concert probably wouldn't have gone ahead.

Some other officers arrived to take care of both Berry and PC Mullins, and Dada and I got to ride in the back seat of the police car. Pappy was driving with PC Taylor alongside in the passenger seat. We drove from the city centre to the arena on the edge of town. We got out of the police car next to where Amasi's tour bus was parked and a security guard pointed us towards a small entrance door round the side of the building.

There were crowds of Amasi fans queuing to get in the main doors or milling around outside. One face I didn't expect to see caught my eye.

"Celeste!" I exclaimed. "You are coming to the concert, then! I thought you hated Amasi."

"Uh... I... I guess she's OK, really." I think the scowl had even slipped from her face.

"Why do you always say that I'm immature for liking her, then?" I was feeling brave. I should have questioned her before. Celeste looked up at her older sister who was giving a disapproving look. She glanced down at the floor and then back at me.

"I'm sorry. I suppose I thought I'd seem older or smarter for liking different music. I actually wish I knew as much about Amasi as you do.

It's pretty amazing! I saw you on the news, Demi – that's pretty cool. You really solved it! Where are you going now?" she asked.

"Just returning the guitar so that the concert can go ahead." I nodded towards the shiny instrument in Pappy's hands.

Celeste's jaw hit the floor.

I smiled and walked away between Pappy and Dada.

There was another security guard standing at the small entrance door. He, too, could see what Pappy was carrying and smiled as he stood to one side to allow all four of us through. In the corridor, we were met by the smartly dressed lady who I had seen on stage comforting Amasi all those hours ago at lunchtime. PC Taylor had called ahead and said that we were on our way.

The lady introduced herself as Amasi's manager and guided us through a maze of corridors to a dressing room door. She knocked and put her head round the door to look inside. Then, she opened the door wider and beckoned us in.

I was actually in Amasi's dressing room.

There she was. She looked just like a regular person and yet still so mesmerising. She wasn't ready to go on stage yet and was wearing white joggers with a matching plain white, baggy jumper. Her hair was far from perfect; her make-up wasn't even done. It was like the Amasi from her vlog but mixed with the young Amasi who first started out. She looked so... normal!

Pappy held out the guitar and Amasi's face crumpled with happy tears rolling from her eyes. "Thank you so much!" she said, taking it gratefully and holding it to her chest.

"Well, this is who you have to thank. She always reckoned she was your biggest fan, strutting around the house singing your songs. It was Demi who figured it all out." Pappy's face beamed as he patted me on the back.

My whole body turned to marshmallow. Words formed in my head but my brain couldn't seem to make my mouth move.

"Demi – I don't know what to say. Thank you! You're an absolute star! You're watching the concert, I assume?"

Thankfully, actual words managed to leave my mouth. "Yeah!" I managed. "I couldn't miss it. I've been counting the days!"

"Right, well you make yourself at home here for now. Eat, drink, anything you like. I need to give Nanna and Gramps a quick call to tell them the great news. Oh, and as of now, you're going to be watching from a VIP box!" she beamed.

My marshmallow legs nearly gave way entirely.

It was the most amazing concert. Just before the last two songs, Amasi announced that she was bringing on stage a special guest to join her for 'Steel Yourself'. Everyone must have wondered who it was going to be.

"Without this incredible girl, the concert would

not have happened tonight," she told the entire arena crowd through her microphone. "Please welcome Demi onto the stage."

I can't even properly remember getting from our seats to the stage. My heart was banging like a drum for at least the third time today and echoing in my ears – or maybe that was the actual drummer this time. It was hard to tell! My legs were the wobbliest ever and I wasn't sure my neck was going to hold my head up – it felt so heavy.

My mind swirled but my smile must have stretched from ear to ear. When I reached her, Amasi put her arm around me as she continued talking to the crowd.

I looked out and all I could see were huge, blinding lights shining in my eyes. Somewhere out there, thousands of people were staring back at me, though. I could just about make out a few of them hanging over the metal barrier in the front row. Most were girls my age but I'm pretty sure I recognised a man with a baseball cap that said 'California'. He didn't have his sunglasses on now but his brown, woollen jacket was unzipped and his T-shirt underneath had Amasi's name surrounded by love hearts.

I got to stay up there on stage for the whole song while Amasi performed and, of course, I sang along to every word. After it finished, she asked me on the microphone what I wanted to do when I'm older.

"Well, I've been trying to pick between being a detective who solves crimes or a performer who sings and does some magic," I answered. "But, now, I've decided. I want to be both!"

"I love it!" said Amasi. "Isn't she incredible? Everyone, give it up for Demi!"

From somewhere beyond the blinding lights, the crowd cheered. I walked to the side of the stage and watched from there, where Dada and Pappy were waiting to give me a huge hug.

The opening bars of the final song kicked in: 'Follow Your Dreams'.

I said this morning that this was going to be one of the most exciting Saturdays ever. I knew it would be awesome. I just couldn't possibly have imagined that it would be nearly as awesome as it has actually been. If I have another six hundred, six thousand or even six million Saturdays, they won't beat this one.

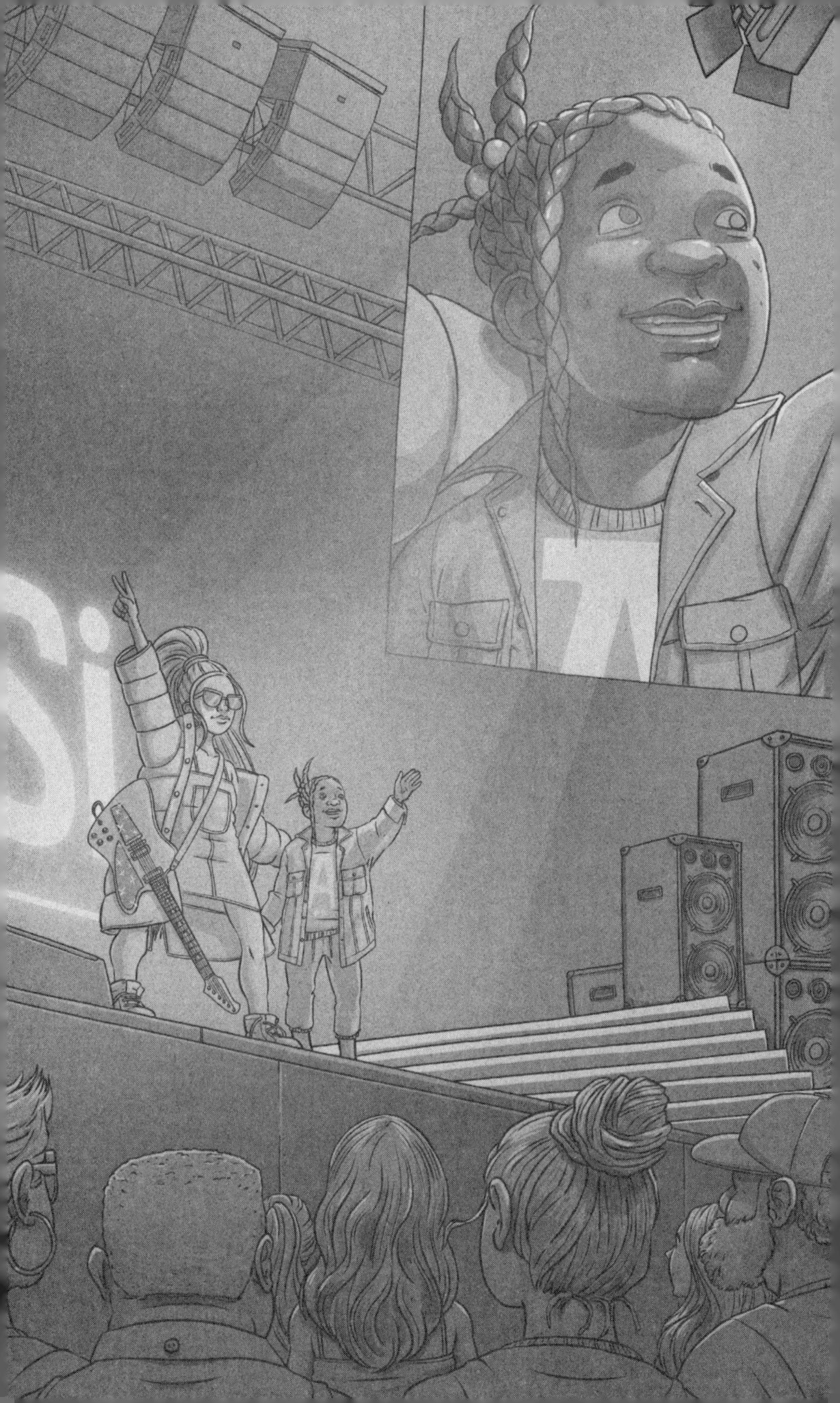

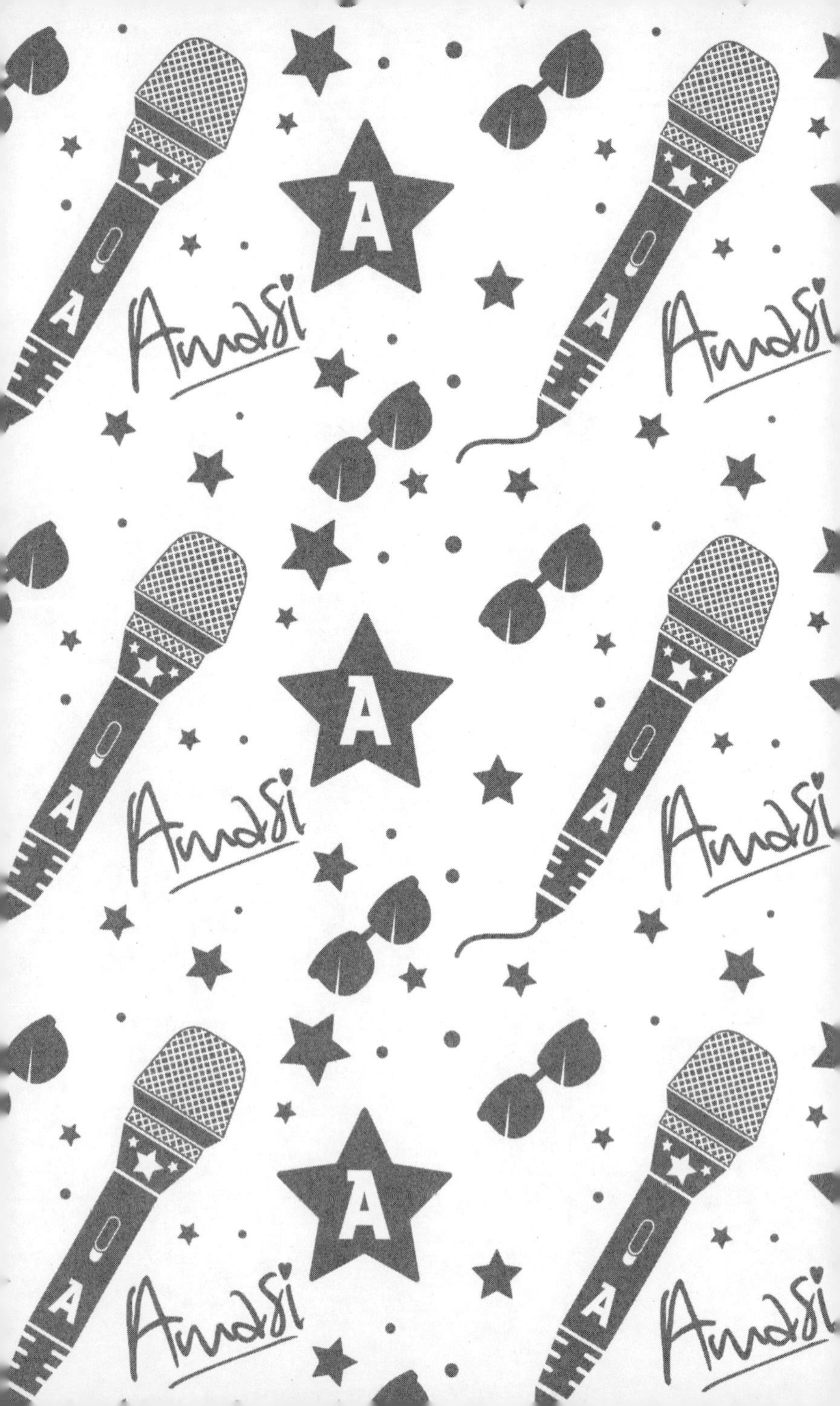

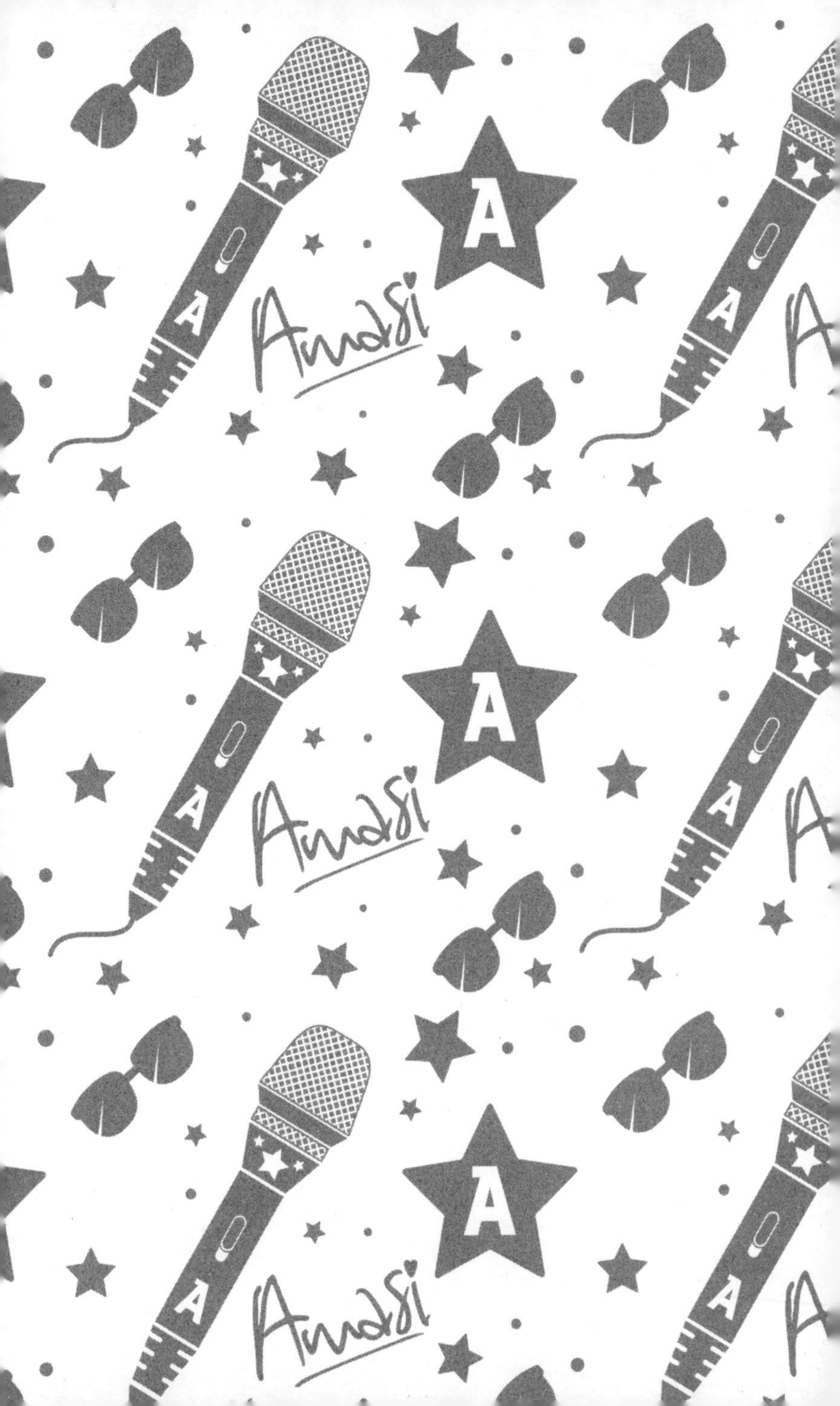

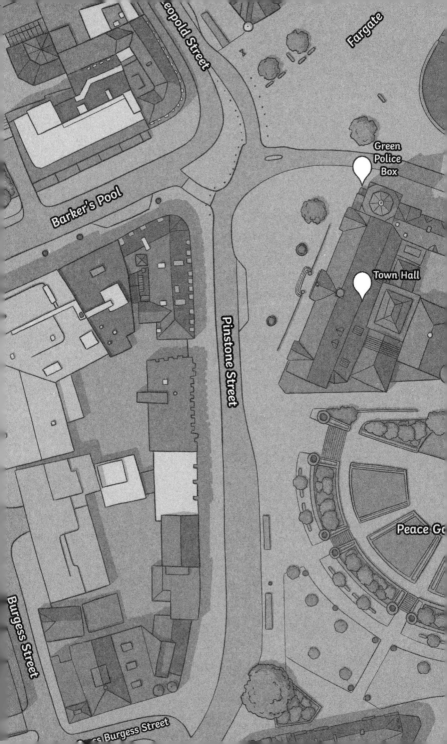

How much can you remember about the story? Take this quiz to find out!

1 What is Amasi's real name?

2 What city do Demi and her dads live in?

3 What is Pappy's job?

4 What famous fictional detective is mentioned in the story?

Answers: 1. Amalie Simpkins 2. Sheffield 3. Police Constable 4. Sherlock Holmes

Challenge

Use the key to work out what the coded words are.

A	B	C	D	E	F	G	H	I	J	K	L	M
1	2	3	4	5	6	7	8	9	10	11	12	13

N	O	P	Q	R	S	T	U	V	W	X	Y	Z
14	15	16	17	18	19	20	21	22	23	24	25	26

Then, unscramble the letters in bold to reveal a bonus word!

1. 4-5-20-5-3-**20**-9-22-5
2. 3-12-**21**-5
3. 19-15-**12**-22-5
4. 8-21-14-3-**8**
5. 23-9-20-14-5-**19**-19
6. 19-21-19-16-**5**-3-20

Discussion Time

 Why is the guitar so important to Amasi?
What do you own that has sentimental value to you?

 Who were the potential suspects in this story?

Do you think Demi was right to leave Dada and investigate the green police box?

What consequences should Berry and his sister face as a result of their actions?

Discover more from Twinkl Originals...

Continue the learning! Explore the library of The Curious Case of the Stolen Show activities, games and classroom resources at twinkl.com/originals.

Welcome to the world of Twinkl Originals!

Board books

Picture books

Longer stories

Books delivered to your door

Enjoy original works of fiction in beautiful printed form, delivered to you each half term and yours to keep!

1 **Join the club** at **twinkl.com/book-club**

2 Sign up to our **Ultimate membership**.

3 **Make your selection** – we'll take care of the rest!

The Twinkl Originals app

Now, you can read Twinkl Originals stories on the move! Enjoy a broad library of Twinkl Originals eBooks, fully accessible offline.

Search '**Twinkl Originals**' in the App Store or on Google Play.

Look out for the next Book Club delivery

Ash is in year six. He loves costumes, lights and smoke machines, and standing centre stage with all eyes on him. However, on the opening night of the school play, it all becomes a little too much and his courage fails him.

Everyone gets nervous sometimes, and Ash is determined to make amends. Soon, though, his year six exams are on top of him and he's convinced that he's going to fail.

Feeling alone and under pressure, Ash reaches out to his friends and family. Can he find the courage to face his exams and find his voice again?

Coming July 2022

Can't wait?
Get the digital version at
twinkl.com/originals

Have you read these Twinkl Originals books?

Leila is tired of the hustle and bustle of life in the ancient Egyptian city of cats until, one day, she comes across a very unusual cat with a very unusual problem. Now, it's a race against time to recover a lost magical item from the depths of the pharaoh's tomb.

Can Leila and her new companion save the city of the cat goddess before it's too late?

It is 1916. A spindly tree stands in No Man's Land during the First World War amid wooden stumps and razor-sharp wire. Hatched into the horrors of war, two birds sit in the tree. Humans live in trenches on either side – but are they friends or enemies?

Can the birds' plan to sing for peace finally see an end to the years of danger?

It's 1941. When cousins Sam and Lily are evacuated out of London to a sleepy seaside hamlet, they hope that they'll find safety. Instead, the two children encounter local hostility, a shifty character sending secret messages, and a treacherous plot.

Can Sam, Lily and their new friends crack the code before hundreds are killed?

When Daisy's school gives her the opportunity to view a charity's rainforest webcam feed in South America, she knows that it's a once-in-a-lifetime experience. What she doesn't expect is an unlikely video-caller with a very serious problem! Follow Pedro the potoo as he explores each layer of the Amazon rainforest.

Will Daisy answer the animals' cry for help?

Visit the online shop to browse the library!

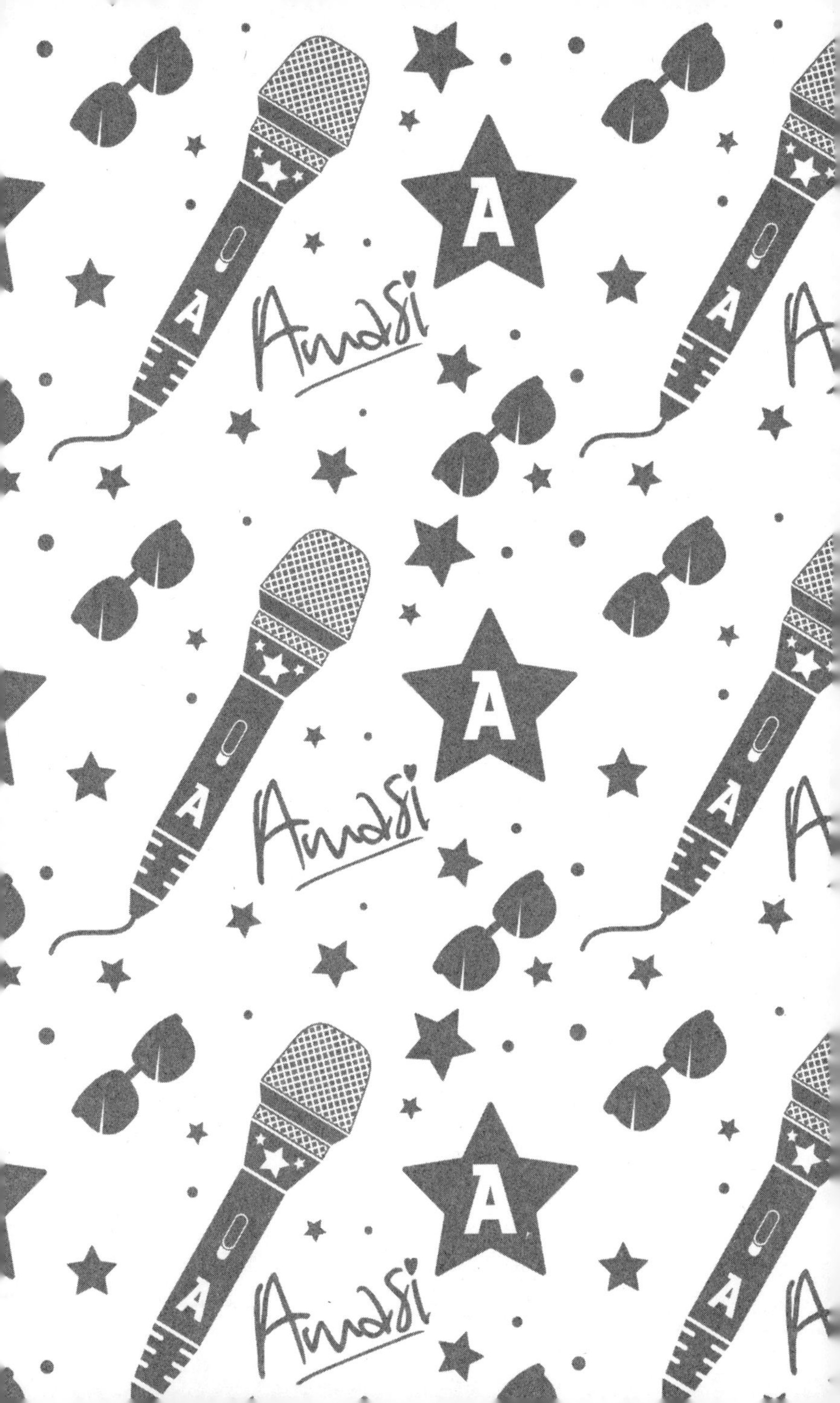